# Street Vices II

# Anthology

## Ms. Pantha Jones

## Avorey Washington,

## Tiara Bland

## Kieshawn Whaley,

## EBAH

## Green-Eyed Puerto Rican

This is a work of fiction. Any references or similarities to actual events, real people, living, or dead, or to real locals are intended to give the novel a sense of reality. Any similarity in other names, characters, places, and incidents is entirely coincidental.
Take Over Publishing LLC
Gary, Indiana 46404

TakeOver Publishing LLC
Gary, In

Paperback ISBN#13 978-0-9824338-7-4

Copyright ©2018 Take Over Publishing LLC
Copyright ©2018 Ms. Pantha Jones
Cover artist: LRB
Editor: Travis VP Fox

# Acknowledgments

## Ms. Pantha Jones

I remember when I put out Respect My Gangsta my acknowledgments were two pages long, it has since then dwindled down. Clarity of what support really is comes with time. With that said, I want to thank all the upcoming authors and seasoned authors for participating and coming through for a Street Vices Anthology 2. I would like to Thank Travis Fox, for taking the time out from his career to aide me in the editing process with some of the stories. Super thanks to Avorey Washington for doing more than his share of work. Thank my family. Mahogany Bang, Donna Williams, Lalita Arnold, Latoya Mabon(for always being my go-to for opinions rather it's test reading or book cover designs). A special shout out for my son Tyrin aka My Cain for allowing me to constantly use his laptop when mine's broke.

## Avorey Washington-

First off, I'd like to thank God for this talent, not sure what I'm really supposed to do with it but I'm thankful for it. I'd like to thank Ms. Pantha Jones for giving me a chance to come outside and play in her literary sandbox. Thanks to my mother and father for me over the top personality. A humble thanks to all my 'wives' ( Tameka, Datianna, Helaynia, Trice, Veronica, Quells and Monique). To my best friend Keith and his family for the continued support. Special thanks to my Dingo brethren, my IUN family, Ms. Davis, the XGW family, my friends, my siblings, my cousins-especially Victoria. My Facebook fam (Aj, Brandy, Talisha, Brandi, Fefe, YoGee Bare, Zoya, Matthew, and

Dawn). And a very anomalous thanks to any and everyone who has ever read any of my work (kakscorner.com)....and then didn't try to have me committed. lol. Love you all."

## Kieshawn Whaley

First, always and forever, I give all praises and thanks to Dr. Henry Clifford Kinley, all the God that there is. I thank Dr. Kinley for giving me this talent and using me as the vessel to write this powerful story. I would be nothing and I am nothing without the living Elohim himself so I give him all of the credit for his will and purpose. Second, I want to give a shout out to my mother who is my rock. Mom, you've done nothing but support me through the ups, downs, ins, and outs. Having a mother like you so strong allows me to see that anything is possible if you have faith. You hold it down and I will forever be grateful and thankful for Dr. Kinley using a vessel like you to show his purpose and his power. I want to shout out my big brother, for always believing in me and being a supporter as well. To all of my friends and family that have been there for me through my journey, I want to say that I love you all and may these words touch you in a way that you always remember that if you have faith anything is possible.

## Tiara Bland-

Thank you, God, for blessing me with the talent. Ms. Pantha Jones for believing in me. My two daughters Ne'Vaeh and Azaria, My son Amir. Mommie does it all for you three!

## E.B.A.H.

Thank you goes to the MOST HIGH, and TakeOver Pub for this opportunity.

**Patricia Pickett**

I heard a mantra once, "No rain no flowers"
And without rain, there are no flowers and without thunder,
there is no rain. I'm very grateful for those thunderstorms
and I'm so thankful for opportunity and my family.

# Demon Knight

# By

# Avorey Washington

**"And my wrath shall wax hot, and I will kill you with the sword, and your wives shall be widows, and your children fatherless."-Exodus 22:24**

**"Who can stand before His indignation? And who can stand up and endure the fierceness of His anger? His wrath is poured out like fire, and the rocks are broken asunder by Him"-Nahum 1:6**

### Chapter 1

Sitting here in the back of this dingy van, gas fumes invade my nose. The cold metal floor gives no comfort to my butt. I've been back here for what seems like an eternity. This piece of shit on wheels has a bad need for shocks, so I feel every bump and turn the driver makes.

One hundred. One hundred and one. One hundred and two.

I pass the time by counting the number of potholes the driver hits. The rate in which he's hitting them, not sure if he's blind as Stevie Wonder or the streets in Gary are that bad. No matter how you call it, this lets me know he's still on the east side of town. The driver talks with the passenger sitting up front.

One hundred and ten. One hundred and eleven.

"I can't believe this shit," the driver says. "One

fucking kid, and a rather chubby fuck at that."

The passenger gives out a chuckle of disbelief. Out of my peripheral, I can see him, and hear him suck his teeth in disgust.

"Hey lard ass," the passenger calls out to me.

Avoiding eye contact, my eyes stay glued to the cold hard metal floor as to not to provoke him further. At this moment I have no idea where I am, or what I'm involved in- so the less reason I give anyone to confront me until I figure things out the better.

One hundred twenty...one hundred twenty-one...one hundred twenty-two.

The passenger insists on having a line of communication with me.

"Hey fat bastard, I got some cookies. You hungry fatty mcfat fuck? I know you hear me, fat cunt."

He calls me every fat bastard, fat fuck and every other name under the sun he could use the adjective 'fat' in-to harness my attention.

"Hey, you fat faggot..."

"Yo man, lay off him," the driver says in my defense trying to ease the situation.

Once he sees I'm not easily baited, and all his insults fell on deaf ears-he turns his attention to his ringing cell phone. The loud irritating voice suddenly turned low and soothing. All of a sudden he tried to sound as easy and laid back as a disc jockey spinning oldies on a Saturday night. Not wanting to hear his weak attempt at what he called game, I continued counting the potholes we hit.

"Yeah baby, I been thinking about you all week", he pauses to let out a creepy laugh. "When it comes to you, I got more 'wood' than a lumber yard. Oh, fo sho. I can show you better than I can tell you. Sheeeeeit. I ain't on nothing later tonight. Just working a little hustle right now. Oh mos def, I can be through later."

One hundred and thirty.

Closing my eyes I see red. Not the pretty version of the color either. Not the red you see when you color kites in coloring books, nor the red that comes to mind when you eat a juicy apple. The dark thick version, like blood.

My mind is a jumble of violent episodes. I hear grunting and screaming-the sound of bones breaking. The sound of bullets whizzing in the air, and the smell of gunpowder. Sounds of someone gasping for breath. The spine-chilling vision of a bullet as it breaks human skin, and hits bone-similar to how a S.W.A.T team kicks in the front door during a raid.

One hundred thirty-seven

Clenching my eyes tighter I can hear someone begging for mercy. Whoever it is, their pleas of being spared falls on deaf ears. I can hear and visualize them taking their last breath. I watch the body drop. The corpse slumps in such a way that it looks like an actor who was bowing before the audience it had just performed in front of.

One hundred forty-five.

My breathing becomes labored as I stand inside my mind watching all this unfold. A few single bullets whiz by me, mere inches from making contact with my skin. The gunman is too far away to make out a description of him. All I see is the flash of light, as the bullets leave the chamber-and seek out their unknown destination.

One hundred fifty.

The gunman pauses long enough to reload. He tosses the empty magazine, reloads and begins again. Five bullets come in my direction together, like a group of angry bees. If I was a betting man, I'd have laid everything on the line to say they were going to make their new permanent home in my flesh. Would've bet you anything these bullets were about to invade my body like the US military does any foreign land it pleases.

One hundred fifty-three.

My attempt at closing my eyes before impact fails. If this was how I was leaving this earth, I sure as hell didn't want to stare my demise in the eye. Everything now is in slow motion, the sound of bullets coming toward me is loud and deafening, like the sound of monster trucks revving.

One hundred fifty-seven.

Shockingly they don't make contact with me, I wasn't

their intended target. The five bullets that I thought were for me- ease right on pass me, like Dorothy, the Tin-Man, the Cowardly Lion, the Scarecrow and Toto eased on down the yellow brick road. Apparently, my body wasn't the wizard they were off to see.

One hundred and sixty.

The brakes squeal as the driver brings the van to a halt. The engine idles for a few seconds before he kills it. The driver begins to give his buddy shit for being on the phone and caking. The passenger pays him no mind as he opens his door. My eyes open, but I don't lift my head.

"Don't even think about getting out" the driver says to me exiting the van. "I'll be right outside."

The passenger was still on the phone running his weak mack. Pretty sure he would have given me a more unique and colorful warning about attempting an escape if he wasn't so preoccupied with trying to get some ass later tonight.

Clenching my fist, I try to put together the last couple of hours. Try to figure out how this morning started off normal. I ate breakfast. Went to school, and as usual tried to survive being a social outcast among the masses of pretty boys, jocks, rich kids and dope boys. But that didn't happen exactly. I went to school, but things changed today. A lot of things changed. In fact, things changed so harshly I was ready to end my life both literally and figuratively.

A few hours ago I was standing on the 4th Avenue Bridge, overlooking the South Shore train tracks. Cars passed by behind me, as I looked at the train tracks below. The yellow and green "Willows Apartment Complex" neon sign shined bright, but not bright enough to consume the darkness in my head. My thoughts were as black and cold as the rocks and train track some fifteen or twenty feet below me.

After the day I had, I was ready to jump. But I didn't, not because the will to live came back with a vengeance. My meeting with the unknown was interrupted by a damsel in distress. That's the problem with society, interruptions, and distractions. It's gotten to the point where a man can't commit suicide alone in peace.

I'll spare you the long story, and give you the short version. Just as I was about to swan dive to my sudden demise, a car swerves nearly missing me. The tire had blown, or rather had been shot out and the driver had lost control of the car. The vehicle crashes through the guardrail, slides down the small hill and comes to a rest in someone's front yard.

Making my way down the hill, I approach the upside down car. No one is inside. The homeowner comes out looking around and shouting at me. I try and explain it's not my car, he doesn't listen. Further up Clark Road, I see the driver trying to run. They're not making good time, due to the minor limp they have.

I start a mild jog in the direction of the driver, just as a black SUV a screeches hard at the broken guardrail. They see the homeowner ranting at me, look in my direction and then spot the driver. Three of them stand there, like Gods on Mount Olympus. A quick flash-and the homeowner fall back to the ground. Headshot, he's probably dead. I run harder.

I wind up catching up to the driver, which turns out to be a classmate. But not just any classmate, the valedictorian of my class LeChell. She explains to me about how she thought she was just dropping off a package for her boyfriend Chauncey, but soon found out she was at a drug deal gone bad. We run until we find someone who was dumb enough to leave their car in the middle of Clark Road running. A crazy car chase ensues through the streets of Gary. I made the assumption our pursuers weren't too pleased about her survival with the way they gave chase.

The chase ends with me crashing into the now abandon Emerson High School. I disarm the three men, only to run into a group of 5 more with loaded guns. We get tossed in the back of the van, and I have no idea where the hell I am.

Looking at my fist, I can see the damaged skin on my knuckles. Streaks of dried blood, and even what appears to be a few bite marks. Swearing to myself as I open and close my fist trying to survey if anything is broken.

"Are you ok?" a soft feminine voice whispers.

"Yeah, right as the rain in Spain," I say while checking out my other fist.

LeChell is her name. LeChell Tomeia Payne, and like me, she's a seventeen-year-old high school student. We're both black, or if you want to be anal and all politically correct-African American. Both of us were born and raised in Gary, Indiana, and attend the same high school. That's where the similarities between us cease.

"Listen, Demon," she pauses long enough to make her way to my side of the van. "You didn't have to help me, but I appreciate it."

Before I could say anything the van door swings open, and both of us are snatched out. We're escorted by a group of 10 guys in suits into the Gary State Bank Building on the corner of 5th and Broadway. The loud jazz music of John Coltrane's "Blue Train" evades my ears.

The Centier Bank is closed, but one of Gary' finest sits at a little desk. As the men escort us in, he doesn't look up. "The Centennial at 504" is jumping, looks like a high-class event. I can see fancily dressed waiters serving drinks and finger foods. A black tux affair with some of the big wigs of Lake County, I think I may have even seen the mayor. Lights that were mellow, yet colorful and inviting all reflected off a giant ice sculptor on a nearby food table. Before I could get a better view, the doors were rudely closed on us as we waited for the elevator.

My captors weren't as sharp as the party guests I observed. No flashy tuxedos, just what appeared to be clearance rack suits. Nothing as flashy as you would get from Tom Olesker's in the Village when it was open. We get off on the third floor and are led to a rather swanky art deco office. The office was laid out, you would think some fancy big wig cut deals here.

A custom-made oak desk sat at an angle in the corner, with two plush chairs in front of it. LeChell and I were forcefully made to sit in those chairs. Behind us was a decent sized boardroom table, where the ten goons who escorted us sat. Looking out the window to my left, there's a good view of the makeshift Park and Town Square across the street.

At this point, I wish I was on that "Blue Train" in the song, or any train right now escaping. Be it the "Midnight Train to Georgia" Gladys Knight sang about. "The Last Train to Clarksville" by The Monkees. Shit! I'd even take a "Yellow Submarine" with the Beatles to get the hell out of here.

Fear crippled me to the point I couldn't focus enough to form logical thought. LeChell was sobbing like no one's business. Mumbling and sobbing, in between a prayer to the man upstairs. They say Jesus is always on the main line. I never really got that saying, it always made him seem like a chatty teenage girl who was on the phone. But at this time, I was hoping he is was the main line or hoping he could hear LeChell calling.

## Chapter 2

Five of the ten goons paced around this office. All looking at me in confusion, snickering. A loud annoying guy walked in, a complete standout. He had mangled dreads, baggy jeans, knock off Gucci flip-flops and a wife beater.

They all eyed me, made jokes and snickered about their dead associates. Made jokes about me looking like a lame. Made comments about me being a husky teenager, and how it looked like I couldn't lose my virginity in a whore house on payday. Each of them randomly walking by me and jumping at me wondering if I would flinch. And when I didn't flinch or even so much as blink, I could hear their egos begin to cry like a child with a skinned knee.

"Do you know what they call me in these streets, huh?" the goon in the wife beater said.

When I didn't answer, he got in my face, grabbing it roughly. He asks me again while squeezing my jaws. I blinked a few times due to his horrid breath. Never in my life had my nostrils been raped by halitosis of this nature. It was almost an injustice to halitosis to call it that. The only thing that came to mind to describe the odor, was like he had a homeless man with his shoes off-living in his stomach.

"Fat boy...they call me Tic-Tac in these G.I. Streets," he said with great accomplishment.

"I can't comprehend why," I say through clenched teeth. "Judging by the smell of your breath, you've never had one."

"Hey we don't attack our guests", a smooth deep baritone voice said. Seconds later, the origin of the voice was sitting behind the desk in front of us. He was a tall, well-tailored and well-spoken dark skin individual. As he placed his hat on this desk, he reaches for a cigar and gently smiles at me. It was as if Billy Dee Williams had a clone.

Tic Tac was angry and emotional. Apparently, two of the three men I had killed earlier were his brothers. The well-dressed man listened as Tic Tac ranted, verbally cursing me and occasionally shoving me. Judging by how the others got in line when he entered, it was safe to say he was the one who pulled their strings. Tic Tac slapped me, and the man behind the desk threatened that if he touched me again, his mother would have to bury three sons and not two.

"I'll cut to the chase. This young lady I know. She is the girlfriend of one of my employees. Ms. Payne also attends the same church as me. But I haven't the pleasure of meeting you Mister...," the Billy Dee clone said.

He nodded toward me waiting for me to introduce myself, but I was too emerged in his mysterious facade to speak. I wasn't freaked out as much, as I wanted to know who I was dealing with. Game recognizes game, and crazy does the same. If I had a brown belt in crazy, I'm sure this guy had a third-degree black belt- at the very least.

There was a vibe, a dark one that he was giving off, that most people would overlook because of his expensive suit and welcoming grin. He looked like the type to murder you in the middle of dinner and continue eating his meal while watching you slowly die for his own entertainment.

I would have remained in disgust and curious awe of this man, unluckily for me, Tic Tac was there. He forcefully removes my wallet, tossing my identification to his boss.

The head man in charge looks over my ID carefully, and carefully places my wallet in the middle of his desk with care.

"My name is Troy Mathius McCall. And according to your identification, you're Demon Knight. Now is that pronounced Demon as in angels and demons? Or is it Demon as in Demond?", he said asked while puffing on his cigar.

Still unable to gather enough nerve to speak, Tic Tac loses his cool with me thinking I'm purposely being disrespectful. He grabs me by the back of my neck and shakes me, Mr. McCall doesn't approve. Before I could even react, Tic Tac was dead on the floor with a bullet in his head courtesy of his boss. LaChell lets out a minor shriek.

Our eyes met, as Mr. McCall smiles and put the smoking gun back in his drawer. There was a silencer on the gun, so there was no loud gunfire to disrupt the function downstairs. Waving his hand and nodding three of the goons in suits carried away their fallen man in arms.

"Now that's four men you've cost me, Mr. Knight. Something must be done about that kid," he pauses as LaChell's boyfriend Chauncey walks in.

Chauncey was light skinned, six feet tall, and the star of our high school's basketball team. He was every girl in my class's idea of hot. The epitome of sexy. He was well liked among students and faculty. He was the reason I was on the bridge tonight and I wanted to end it all. He also carried secrets with him. Secrets that he wanted to keep unknown by any means. His shock of seeing me suddenly turned into a smug smirk as he buttoned his suit jacket.

A conversation between the two is shared. The gist of it was Chauncey was to deliver a package. He blew it off and entrusted LaChell with it. Not knowing that the buyer was planning to double-cross Mr. McCall, and somehow they figured I was tied in with it. Once it was all sorted, and it proved I was innocent, it was determined that I was a loose end that needed to be tied up.

Moments later Mr. McCall exits the room taking Chauncey with him, leaving me with the remaining goons. Those moments seemed like an eternity on repeat, until they returned.

"I apologize for this unfortunate event in which I am about to present to you, Mr. Knight. Here's the thing. I can't let you leave this building here in good conscience, not knowing if you're a snitch or not."

I want to speak, but he cuts me off before any words can escape my lips.

He continues, "But I'm a fair man. And lucky for you my guests are waiting to be entertained. We have a little game that goes on secretly in this city. A sort of underground fight club. Long story short. I will give you the chance to fight for your life. The chance to fight for your survival tonight. It's simple. My guys will take you to the top floor of this building. And if you can fight by any means and make it down to the fourth floor-and escape to the connected parking garage, where my party guests are waiting, then you can walk out of here."

Smiling warmly he motioned for me to stand, and to follow him. We entered the hallway, took the elevator to the second floor. We step off and head to the left, which leads us to a set of double doors that opens to a wraparound marble balcony overlooking the first floor.

Turning to him I say, "And what's my other option if I don't accept your game of cat and mouse."

Like a politician, he waves to the party guests below with a smile, but mouths to me, "Possibly a long drawn out death. Probably won't even leave enough of you for a casket. I mean you did kill three of my best men. Which is why I'm even curious enough to give you this opportunity."

"So either way I'm a dead man?"

He turns to me, looking me over with a smirk, "No, you're not. But I can make it to where you wish you were dead son."

"How so?"

Putting his hand on my shoulder, I could see the darkness in his eyes illuminate. His grip tightened on my shoulder, keeping me in place.

"Well, how would you like to be the reason everyone in your graduating high school class dies. Including that beautiful young lady in my office."

Nonchalantly I shrug, "I'm not really fond of them anyway no big deal."

"Is that so? So you'd be fine with knowing you could have prevented the deaths of about one hundred innocent kids. You'll sleep well knowing you could have prevented the deaths of possible future lawyers, doctors and lots of other fields. People who could make a difference in this world."

He watches me as the words he said sink in. And for a moment I think about it. All the life's of the people for the last couple of years that have made my life a living hell. In one simple answer, I could end them or be a hero they'd never know about.

"Yeah, I pretty much think I'd sleep peacefully, Mr. McCall. Most of them aren't very good people or smart anyway", I say with a smile.

Pausing for a moment, he turns away from me and looks down at his guests of the party. I can see his jaw clench, and his hand tightens on the marble railing. An unsettling smile overcomes his face as he turns his attention back to me.

"Very well. You don't look like a snitch. So here's how it's going to go, son. You don't have to play my game. You can walk out that front door and never see me again."

"Never see you again, ever?"

He puts his hand on my shoulder and leans in close to me, "Never."

I nod and make my way back to the double doors. I'm almost back in the hallway when I hear.

"You'll never see me again....that is......until you're about to die. But who knows when that will be right?"

Once again that politician smile is on his face as he winks. Before I can march back to him, he's already walking in my direction, he stops directly in front of me.

"Did you just threaten my life, Mr. McCall?"

He laughs, "No my dear boy. I don't make threats." Seriousness owns his facial expressions. "I make promises" His tone of voice changed from friendly to that of an angry parent. "Don't let this suit fool you, I make shit happen young man. You walk out that door tonight. Every kid in your class will die, one by one. Maybe even two at a time until you're the only one left to walk across that stage. I'll make it so you will be the only surviving graduating member of your class. Sounds lonely, doesn't it? And I'll have the media spin it as if you had something to do with it."

At this moment I'm filled with fear to the point all I can say is, "Yeah, ok. Sure."

I can tell by the ever-growing anger on his face, my tone offends him. He shoves me against one of the double doors.

"Son, you must think I'm something to play with. I'm the kind of guy that makes the devil swear when my feet hit the floor. You leave here, you WILL have a hundred deaths on your head. Do you know how many parents would be calling for your head? How many people who would be looking for justice if it was leaked that you had something to do with it?

Mr. McCall leans in closer to me, roughly resting his forearm on my throat, pinning me against the door. I struggled, but for an old man, he was strong. We were eye to eye and I could see the darkness first hand in the windows of his soul. His face was menacing, yet calm-the demeanor he possessed let me know he's probably killed a lot of people.

The expensive cologne he wore invaded my nostrils, as he pulled a switchblade from his suit jacket. He ran the cold blade lightly across my cheek, just enough to draw a pin drop of blood.

"Little niggas from your generation aren't the brightest", he says applying more pressure to my throat. "I see a ton of them dumb shits like Chauncey every day. Selfish and self-absorbed, thinking the world is all about them". He moves the sharp blade mere inches from my right eye, as I struggle to breathe. "But you look like a smart kid, and I'm sure you see the point I'm trying to make right? We should all care for our fellow man. And you have the chance to do that tonight."

He steps back from me and adjusts his suit, while I bend over gasping for air. Standing straight up, I run my hand along my throat. Mr. McCall stands there, one hand in his pants pocket-the other stroking his chin.

"And let's just say you survive and manage to put the pieces back together of your life. You leave for college and find a nice girl to settle down with. Get married and have a kid. You would actually be foolish enough to think it's over and you won. Ha. Not fucking likely. It wouldn't be over. Know why it wouldn't be over? Because I would make sure to fuck with you from afar on a daily. I'd have you looking over your shoulder at every turn. No matter where you went, I would find you. This shit wouldn't be over until you were dead in a box, by my own doing."

And just as quickly as all that anger in his face showed up, it cleared up the same way. It was like how a fast rain storm came and a few moments later, the sun was out bright and shining as if nothing happens. He pulls me from against the door with a smile while smoothing out the wrinkles in my shirt. We stare at each other for what seems like forever.

Without any further words spoken he walks to the elevator and presses the button. Seconds later, it arrives and he motions for me to join him again. Reluctantly I follow and try to squeeze into one corner of the tiny elevator. Even if I was in another country, I would still feel I was too close to this man now. The doors open to the first floor, we both exit and stand face to face.

"Thank you for your time, Mr. Knight. It was definitely an experience."

He stands there like a gracious host smiling, one of his hands in his pocket while the other extended toward the front door letting me know I was excused. I slowly make my way to the door, bumping into a few late arriving guests for his party.

As I get closer to the door I watch my back, unsure of the game he was playing. My hand was on the door handle, as I heard an elevator ding again. Another one of his paid suited goon's steps off the elevator, speaks with him and hands him something. He tosses something in my direction, I flinch as it lands at my feet.

Bending down I pick up my wallet. I check to make sure my ID and everything is accounted for as he presses the elevator button again. I watch him step on, and then I turn to walk out the door. Before I could step outside to freedom, he calls out to me again.

"One more thing, Mr. Knight. Be sure to tell your grandmother, Odessa, that Little Troy said hello.

When he mentions my grandmother a wave of nausea hits me, but I don't vomit. He puts his index and middle finger to his temple and gives me a salute.

"Be seeing you around, son."

And just like that, he disappears into the elevator again.

## Chapter 3

I can't breathe right now. It was like literally all the air had been sucked out of me. Clutching my chest, I make it to one knee and start a nasty coughing spell. I felt like the black girl in "Nightmare on Elm Street Four" when Freddy killed her by sucking the air out of her by kissing her.

A few more late guests walk in and attempt to give me aide. Waving them away, I pull myself up assuring them I'm fine. When I'm able to breathe normally again, I walk to the elevator and get off on the second floor. I find him in the same spot we were before, on the balcony looking at his guests, but this time he's talking with one of his employees.

When he sees me standing in the doorway he claps his hands with a smile, pointing both index fingers at me.

"Looks like we got ourselves a ball game folks," he says playfully patting his employee on the back.

He nods and a few of his employee's on the first floor lead the party guests to the main lobby. We, on the other hand, take an elevator to the tenth floor, accompanied by three of his goons. We step onto the cold marble floor of the semi abandon looking floor.

"The rules are simple Mr. Knight. Survive by any means. On floors four through ten, I will have an undisclosed number of my men. You make it to the fourth floor there is a connecting tube to the parking garage, where I and my esteemed guests will be watching. There are cameras all over the building. And the office phones have been disconnected in case you get any ideas to call for help."

Exhaling and looking around I ask, "How do I know when each floor is clear of men? And how in the world is anyone not going to call the cops with all the shooting? Your men have guns, I don't."

He laughs at me like I had asked a childish question.

"You have no idea who really runs this city, do you? That's cute."


"Mr. Knight, good luck. And try to make this interesting. People are gambling their hard earned money on you to see how long you last. Oh, by the way, watch the fire alarm lights. When you see them blink white, that indicates the floor is clean. And I'll even give you a ten-minute head start to prepare yourself."

Mr. McCall and his three goons entered the elevator. He watches me, smiles vindictively as our eyes lock as the door closes. Once the door was closed I ran like the devil was hot on my tail. I tripped over my own feet, fumbling into one of the abandoned offices.

Knocking over boxes of files, rambling through file cabinets and trying to get in locked desk drawers, I was looking for anything that could be of use. I had explored two of the dusty offices and had found nothing of real use. Only things I came across were loose paper clips, and a shit load of files in boxes-unless I was going to paper cut them to death I was fucked.

By the look of the offices, it was clear that they hadn't been used in a while. My hands were covered in dust by this time, and if I didn't find anything soon they would be covered in blood. My own blood that is.

His men have guns, which I'm sure they wouldn't

hesitate to you use-so I needed to balance the playing field.

Rummaging through half vacated offices I felt like I was in a video game like 'The Last of Us'. Searching for anything that would be useful in my survival. I turned over moving boxes filled with files, pulled out desk drawers and pushed over file cabinets searching for a miracle. After going through ten offices, a pair of scissors, two razor-sharp letter openers, and a stapler were the best I could find.

The elevator dinged, as I left out one of the offices, letting me know my ten-minute head start had expired. Having only explored only a third of the floor for weapons, I took what I found and snuck into a nearby restroom.

The restroom was dimly lit. I quickly unscrewed the light bulbs as my adversaries walked around talking among themselves and laughing. Their shoes either clicking or squeaking on the marble floor-they gave no fucks about the element of surprise. Putting the bulbs in the sink, I rush to one of the stalls and stand on the toilet seat hoping it can support my weight.

Darkness, I'm surrounded by it as I try and calm my

breathing. My thoughts are rampant, running wild like so many stray dogs in this city. I'm playing devil's advocate about why should I even fight anyway, I mean a few hours ago I was going to commit suicide. While the debate of sink or swim goes on in my head, the door suddenly bursts open and I tense. The light switch flicks a few times and he swears when no light comes on. Mumbling to himself about having to piss, he walks in cautiously. I can see the tactical light on his pistol move back and forth as makes his way into the bathroom.

Once he feels he's safe, he turns off the tactical light and holsters his weapon. He struggles with his zipper a moment before I hear the sound of him urinating. I ease off the toilet as he moans in relief, adrenaline kicks in, letter opener in my hand. Swiftly leaping from the stall, one hand goes over his mouth and the other delivers the letter opener to his throat. Driving it in deeper and twisting, feeling the liquid warmth on my person, some of it is blood squirting and the other one, more than likely piss. The others have no idea they are one man down.

The first thing I do is go for his gun, using the tactical light I search his person for anything that could be helpful. A retractable baton, switchblade, and an extra magazine of ammo is all I find. I know it sounds petty, and possibly pointless-but I even cleaned out the cash in his wallet.

Before leaving the restroom, I go through the extra trouble of propping my pursuer's corpse on a toilet. By my calculations, if I had any chance of surviving, the element of surprise needed to be to my advantage as long as possible. Easing into an office directly across from the restroom, I leave the door cracked, just so I can hear if anyone is coming. Quietly scavenging and finding nothing, as footsteps echo on the marble floor, they get closer pausing at the restroom.

Making my way to the door with the baton, I watch as another peer back and forth, his attention split between going in the restroom or coming into the office I'm in. He chose the restroom. While he's distracted by the lack of light I rush him from behind, bash his head in repeatedly. I let the baton and his skull become best friends, and feel specs of blood fly in my face. Once I'm certain he's dead I search him, find a Mark 19 desert eagle and a Ruger SR1911, both with suppressors and an extra magazine for both.

Just as I had done with his friend, he sat on a porcelain throne now. Leaving the restroom, I catch a glimpse of myself in the mirror due to the light from the hallway. Someone else's DNA splattered on my face, blood specs that gave the appearance of a tattoo or that I had freckles. More blood on my hands as if I were wearing red gloves. For a moment I'm lost in the darkness staring back at me. They say eyes are the window to the soul, and I surely didn't recognize who or what was staring back at me.

More echoes of footsteps bring me back to the here and now, causing me to lose the staring contest with the man in the mirror. Without thought, I ease toward the footsteps, pull the trigger four times, two bullets to the back of the head for each man. Searching their corpses, I come up with nothing and head around to the elevator. I see the white light on the fire alarm, I breathe a sigh of relief as I press the elevator button.

The elevator doors open on the ninth floor, and things get interesting. There were five of them, laughing and joking-no one expected me to make it off the previous floor. Grabbing the closest one to me and using him as a shield, I fire at his comrades, as they return fire. Rushing forward and crashing into an office, I drag the corpse with me for cover as I tumble over a desk.

Gunfire ceases, in that time I reload the desert eagle and listen. Vaguely I can hear from my human shields earpiece they were going to try and flank me. Since the element of surprise is no longer mine I grab the earpiece and radio so I could at least try and stay one step ahead of them. Slowly I peered over the desk, ahead of me the bullet-ridden office doors creaked. Light from the hallway seeped through the bullet holes onto the carpet. Looking to the left and right I see doors leading to connecting offices.

From what I was hearing on the radio, I was outnumbered and pinned down. Their plan was for two guys to come from the left side, one was to be standing at the entrance and the last gunman to play back up coming from the right side.

As a ploy, I remove the silencer from the desert eagle, and before they can get in position I fire shots at the entrance door as a distraction, hoping I killed that one-as I ran to the right adjoining office. The solo gunman on the right wasn't quite ready, his gun jammed and he ran. I gave chase firing until I was out. Out of desperation, I threw the gun, it winged him in the back of the head giving me enough time to tackle him.

We struggle as punches are exchanged, both of us trying to get the advantage. The Ruger falls from my belt during our tussle, he sees a chance and lunges for it. I pull out the switchblade, stabbing him in his leg repeatedly before I stab him twice in the neck-and make his temple the blades final resting place.

While trying to catch my breath I hear on the radio his back up are coming my way. Quickly I grab the Ruger, remove the silencer and fire at the office door in front of me. As I kick the door in, I hear gunshots and footsteps. Before they cut the corner, I slip into the office that's behind me. As I attach the silencer, they did just as I assumed and walked into the office where I had shot the door. Four more bullets find a vacancy in the back of two skulls.

As I was about to search all three corpses, I hear a voice in pain on the radio. Sounds like he's choking on his own blood, as he warns the others on the eighth floor that I was on my way. While listening I creep back around toward the elevator. Cutting the corner I see him, slumped against the marble wall coughing and bleeding profusely.

Before he knew it I was there and it was over. The bullets parted his head like Moses did the Red Sea. The plain white lifeless marble had been brought to life with brain matter and blood. I stared at the wall, stared at my work-my creation. The feeling of being in an upscale and classy art gallery overcame me as I tried to create an image from the blood splatter.

The others on the lower level had been warned, so I had to play this smart. I sure as hell wouldn't be as lucky as I was on this floor if I took the elevator. Thanks to the snitch on the radio, I'm pretty sure they would be covering all four elevators.

Dragging all five bodies to the middle of the lobby, I check them finding nothing of any real use. No extra ammo, just a few stainless steel blades. Grabbing the assault rifle which the radio snitch was holding, I then called the elevators to my floor. Taking cover as they dinged announcing their arrival. To my shock, they were empty, which means they were camped out and waiting.

I put the emergency hold on all the elevators to buy me time. The left two elevators I loaded with two bodies each, the first elevator on the right I put the last body in- leaving the last elevator empty. If this was going to work, I had to time this perfectly. Sending each elevator to the tenth floor, before it was to arrive on the eighth floor. This gave me enough time to make my way back around the corner to the take the stairs.

Except for the buzzing of an exit sign with bad wiring that blinked on and off, the stairwell was pitch black and dusty. I made my way onto the lower floor without a problem and crept up on them as they were waiting by the elevators. I counted maybe five or six voices talking, really couldn't tell. But all got quiet as the elevators all dinged and arrived just seconds after each other. Soon as the doors opened they all opened fire, which was my cue to pop from behind the corner and unload.

## Chapter 4

Bullets flew like birds as they exited the assault rifle, finding new homes in the flesh of those who expected me to be getting off the elevators. No way in hell, they were going to make any of those elevators a temporary metal coffin for me.

As I check the magazine on my rifle, someone gets the drop me. He gets a good grip around my throat like a boa constrictor. The more I struggle the more air I waste. With the last of my energy, I make a desperate attempt to get free. I make my way to the nearest wall, push off it with both my legs hard enough-causing him to crash backward with me in tow, through the glass of an office door.

He screams as his calf is caught on the jagged glass of the door. I crawl further into the office on all fours, hacking and coughing trying to get air in my lungs. Once I'm a coherent and functioning enough, I grab a stapler and bash his skull in. Not only was he giving me a headache from screaming, but I also wasn't sure how many more guys were on this floor-and didn't need him being a beacon.

Winded, I crawled back to the dark part of the office. Eventually made it to sitting in a chair when my strength came back a little more. My left hand ached, I could feel shards of glass in it. After searching the desks, eventually, I found a first aid kit and mirror. I did what I could for my hand, given my current circumstances. Doused it with alcohol and removed the glass with tweezers and covered the gash with gauze and an ace bandage.

Searching the desk I was sitting at, I found a bottle of gin. Taking a few swigs, once again I look in the mirror. I see the same person as I did before on the tenth floor, except his eyes were darker and lifeless. My eyes were the color of death, and I wanted to go home. I shouldn't be here, I should be laid out on the Clark Road train tracks dead. But I choose to be a good Samaritan, try and save a life. As the saying goes, 'no good deed goes unpunished', and what I was in now-definitely was a punishment.

I was in pain and blinded by rage. A fiery wrath had

been building in me, and it was time I let loose. I had all this adrenaline pumping, all cylinders going. I was so anxious to get this over with that I stormed out my hiding spot toward the stairs. I was tired of this game, if I was dying tonight it would be on my terms. Recklessness and abandonment take over, and I'm no longer thinking clearly- maybe that's why I didn't see the guy who jumped me with a baton as I exited the office.

He brought me to one knee the way the baton struck me across my back. From there he got me in a chokehold with it. We danced down the hallway, bumping against the wall and struggling against one another. Clawing at his eyes wasn't working, nor trying to headbutt him. Desperate times call for desperate measures. With my assailant on me like stink on shit, I throw myself into the door leading to the stairwell. We tumble down the stairs, I remember to tuck my head and use him as a shield to cushion the fall down the hard cold concrete steps.

Rolling off him, I can see he landed awkwardly and broke his neck. Despite him taking the brunt of the tumble my body still aches. Taking the pistol in his belt, I scoot to the corner of the stairwell-keeping an eye on the door leading to the seventh floor. Using the wall as an aide I stand up, shake it off as best I can and keep moving.

The seventh floor has been completely gutted out. Nothing but construction tools and materials lying around exposed drywall and beams. Walls had been knocked down, the fluorescent lights flickered like the stairwell exit sign-it felt like I was in a horror movie.

A single guy is staring out a window admiring the view of Fifth Avenue. Probably looking at all the people showing up at the Genesis Center in their Sunday's best on a Wednesday night to step. Three shots to the head and his final thoughts are displayed on the window. Taking some heavy duty electrical cords, I tie them together making a makeshift rope. One end I tie to a beam, the other goes around the neck of the corpse.

His blood and brain matter on the window look like an angry version of the Sesame Street character Elmo. Out of respect, I shoot the next window instead-and toss the dead body out of it. I can hear someone down below scream, as the body dangles like a worm on a hook. A couple of cars screech-some don't stop in time causing an accident.

"Hey folks don't worry, we're just hanging out is all", I say while laughing. My plan was to get the cops here by any means, no way in hell this wouldn't get them here. Reveling in my victory was cut short as I was grabbed and literally flung backward. Before I can recover I'm punched by what feels like a brick and flung around through some drywall.

With the aid of a nearby scaffold I manage to stand up, nothing is broken but my ribs hurt like hell. Turning I see what appears to be a brother at least six foot four, with the body of the incredible hulk and Michael Clark Duncan face. It was like looking at a huge gorilla in a suit.

He charges at me and I move just in time for him to go head first into the scaffold. While he's stunned I search for something to take down this behemoth, especially with little to no places to hide. My only options in reach are a claw hammer and a nail gun. A fast shot to the back of his head with the hammer stuns him even more, giving me enough time to use the nail gun to nail his hands to the wood planks of the scaffold.

I left big man stretched out and nailed like Jesus on cavalry, even nailed his feet to the floor for good measure. There was one more poor soul on this floor, he got off one good shot that grazed my shoulder. I, on the other hand, got off a few nails that got him in the eye, groin, and leg. He howled like a wounded dog, so I did him a favor and fired off a few more nails to his skull.

The game was coming to a close because the entire sixth floor was vacant. The fifth floor was under construction just like the seventh floor but had more places to hide. The lone foot soldier here met his untimely death via buzz saw. I check him for ammo, grab his shotgun and make my way to the fourth floor.

My sweep of the fourth floor left me with four more casualties. I had lost track of how many people I had killed tonight, but I know I racked up a hell of a tab. Good business was made for the Grim Reaper, I just hope when my time comes he remembers this-and makes it comfortable for me.

The office I was hiding in had a clear view of the tube that leads to the parking garage. Placing the shotgun on the desk as I sat down, I was shocked that even with a dead body hanging out the window I heard no police sirens. I had endured this house of horror, and now all I had to do was walk through a set of double glass doors. I was exhausted as I walked out of the office, which would explain why I never saw the next hit coming.

The punch sent me flying, I landed behind the desk. If not for the wall and floor breaking my fall, I surely would be on the sidewalk below, or at least that's what the pain is making me believe. Peering over the desk I see the big man I had encounter and left, nailed like Jesus.

"The guy you tossed out the window. That was my cousin", he says while taking off his tux jacket.

"Well, apparently I got this whole friends and family thing going on. You know kill one family member, and kill a few more for free."

He's not amused at my statement and begins taking

off his shirt. His hands are still bleeding, I can only imagine the pain from ripping free. Using the wall and window for support I stand up and lean against them. The blood drips in thick strands like syrup from his balled fists.

"They call me Apple Jax", he says while pounding his fist together. Specs of blood fly on his chest as he frowns at me.

Grabbing the shotgun off the floor I say, "Well you about to be applesauce bitch." Pulling the trigger repeatedly only to find the gun is jammed. Mr. Jax charges at me with a smile, making his intent clear.

At the last moment, I dodge using his own momentum against him. Crashing head first the through the window he winds up cutting his own throat, I could see glass shards exiting his neck. Using the shotgun to balance myself, I watched as blood flowed down the shattered glass, creating a puddle on the floor. His body jerked, he fought to hold on to the mortal coil.

"We had a breakthrough today. And made some glass shattering progress, glad we could have this talk."

Chuckling to myself at my attempt at humor, I feel his vice-like hand grab my throat. Mr. Jax was not ready to leave this world, either that or he wanted to take me with him. For a man bleeding like a gutted pig, his strength was insane. I swing the shotgun at the window causing a few huge blades of glass to fall, stabbing his neck and piercing his skull. Just be safe I beat his back with the butt of the shotgun, driving him further on the jagged glass.

Battered, bruised, but not broken-I make that long walk down the tube to the connecting parking garage. A few of the party guests are shocked that I survived, others are upset at the money they had lost. Very few were cheering about the money they had won. I grab a flute of champagne as one of the servers walk by and proceed to find a chair and rest my aching body.

Looking around among the crowd I see a lot of the Lake and Porter counties political powerhouses.

"Well Mr. Knight I see you survived", Mr. McCall says while clapping slowly.

Before I could say anything, Chauncey was already taking off his suit jacket and shirt.

"Now the fun is just about to begin Demon."

Tossing the empty champagne glass, I say "Now I have to fight you, Chauncey? Sure, give me a minute to catch my breath and die-and I'll be right with you."

A few of the snobs laugh, Chauncey gets offended and charges at me. Too tired to block fully I wind up taking most of his punches. The advantages go back and forth as we tussle, the guests pretty much make a circle around us.

My body is heavy, hurts to throw a punch. It's taking just about all my energy to stand up, let alone defend or fight back. I throw a punch and he dodges it, winds up behind me and gets me in a choke hold.

"You know Demon...", Chauncey whispers in my ear. "...after you saw me today in the boy's locker room getting head from the captain of the football team, my plan was to make your life a living hell, but now with this situation, I can just kill you and my secret will be safe."

"I wasn't going to tell anyway", I manage to grunt.

"Well, one can never be too sure these days. Just know when you die, I'm going to have a little fun with you before you get disposed of."

He did a sing-song hum in my ear and giggled as he applied more pressure. My futile attempts at elbowing him only made me fade quicker. He continued taunting in my ear until I pulled out the second letter opener I had stashed in my pocket and stab his thigh. I keep stabbing until he lets go, he hobbled backward in retreat but I continued. Tripping over himself, he gave me time to grab him and get in a few lethal stabs to his stomach. I just about finish him off just like I did the first guy in the bathroom when a gun fires.

Turning around I see Mr. McCall with a pistol pointed in my direction. At this moment I have no shame. I played his game and won. I killed three of his top guys, and a shit load of his lackeys tonight. Plus as an added bonus I almost killed my bully, so right now I'm all aces.

So if this is my final moment I'm going out on my terms. I'm so out of it right now, my vision is blurry and I'm seeing double. I was trying to raise my middle finger, but I

don't think I had the strength to do so. I take a step

forward, and suddenly I'm falling and everything goes black.

## Chapter 5

### THREE HOURS LATER

The sounds of humming machinery and beeping wake me. Everything on my body hurts, my nerve endings are on fire. It hurts to even open my eyes, but judging by the beeps, I'm in a hospital and not dead. The room is dark except for the small bit of moonlight that shines through.

Suddenly I hear someone clear their throat.

"Nice to see you're awake kid."

It's Mr. McCall, he steps out the shadows and into the moonlight.

"After what I saw tonight, I'm here to offer you an opportunity. You are definitely a demon son, but I'll refer to you as DK. A little 'dream killer', that's what you are. Because had you killed Chauncey tonight-everyone in Gary who has ever dreamed about any of our high school teams every winning state again-would have been killed by you. Not to mention what you did to some of my men earlier. But for now, I'll leave you my card. Get back to me when you get released. I'll foot the bill."

He places the card on my food tray, no other words are spoken. He leaves my room. Leaves me alone to heal. Leaves me with my scars, both mentally and physically. Leaves me with these nightmares of what happened tonight. Every time I close my eyes, the whole night replays. So I just lay there in the darkness, staring out the window, trying to figure out how to put these unleashed demons in back into the box.

# Pride

# By

# Ms. Pantha Jones

## Chapter 1

I read once online that, "The sin of pride is the ultimate sin. It was this sin, we're told, which transformed Lucifer, an anointed cherub of God, the very "seal of perfection, full of wisdom and perfect in beauty," into Satan, the devil, the father of lies, the one for whom Hell itself was created. We're warned to guard our hearts against pride lest we too "fall into the same condemnation as the devil."

It was the sin of pride which first led Eve to eat of the forbidden fruit. In Genesis, we read, "Then the serpent said to the woman, 'You will not surely die. For God knows that in the day you eat of it your eyes will be opened, and you will be like God, knowing good and evil.' So when the woman saw that the tree was good for food, that it was pleasant to the eyes, and a tree desirable to make one wise, she took of its fruit and ate. She also gave to her husband with her, and he ate." And who do you think was that serpent of old who first introduced Eve to this sin of pride? It was none other than the devil himself, eager to share his condemnation with others.

## Chapter 2

The sin of pride plagues mankind daily, the thin line between being prideful and taking pride in something can be deadly confusing. It can be a demise of your soul, but in the streets, it can be the demise of your life. Standing up for yourself and what you believe in can be honorable but when your life and your family's lives are the consequences of your pride it can be considered foolish in the streets. Especially when the reign of terror in your hood is being conducted by the Devil's spawn. This is the story of Isaiah Villarosa's pride.

Captain Villarosa was a highly respected member of the community. Noble in character on paper, he dedicated his life to protect the streets of Lake County, Indiana. It wasn't because he wanted justice for victims or to stop the crime, it was because his name was connected to the city. And anything his name was connected to he took great pride in it. When the crime rate started going up and the criminals were no longer out on the streets but in the police cars protecting and serving, he desperately needed to get out of Law Enforcement.

"I can't do this anymore," Villarosa confessed to his superior. He sighed as he dropped down into a chair.

"The job getting to you? Or is it because of your parent's death. I am more than willing to give you some time off." She questioned

"No, I don't want my name attached to a fallen city and a corrupted Police department." He told her and laid his badge and gun on the table.

"You know you have two years until you can get your pension?"

"I don't need it. Good luck without me." He said arrogantly walking out.

A sigh of relief with through her body, truth be told Villarosa acted as if anytime a bust was made, he single-handedly did it, then when his department fucked up he wanted no parts of the scandal. He was arrogant and prideful.

Villarosa shot out of the office without so much as a goodbye. Due to his parent's death, he was left a hefty sum of money, which left him with his nose in the air. No more dealing with this bullshit. "No more dealing with you corrupt ass mother fuckers." He screamed as he left the Government building.

The money that he inherited he bought real estate, one, in particular, was a nightclub that he named Villarosa. He was the type that demanded respect and gave respect. For years, there was an understanding between and the Locals in East Chicago, Indiana and him. A couple of years had rolled by without so much as a robbery from the thugs around the way.

However, when this new breed of criminals started patronizing his club demanding to let their Boss wash money in his club. He refused like a gentleman the first time. Their Boss decides if Villarosa wasn't going to join him he was going to make sure his goons beat him, by terrorizing his establishment. They tried everything, even tried to tax him money to stop the goons from destroying his business every weekend.

## Chapter 3

Isaiah Villarosa desperately tried to maneuver out of his restraints as he watched the masked men fondled his wife. The pain and sheer terror on India's face tore at his heart. Two Armalite AR-15 rifles, as well as two infrared red 9mm automatics, were the weapons the five young thugs armed themselves with.

It was the late 80's the crack era, the era of death for the oath of honor amongst thieves. The children of the 70's were grown-up and teaching the 80's babies that the only thing that made sense in America was making cents, dollars, money. By any means necessary.

And for the 80's babies violence was the means. Kangols, dookie, chains, fat lace Adidas and Adidas sweatsuits, guns and crack cocaine-filled vials going from hand to hand by the lost block boys in the ghetto. Lost souls that believe in order to survive they had to stop somebody else from surviving. Even if the man was just a civilian in the streets. And standing right before him was the poster child for all of this. Tango.

"Don't you spit that shit out." he peered down at India while holding his dick. With his dick still hard he entered her pissed filled mouth.

"Oooh, Damn Villarosa your bitch gives good head." Tango peeked over his shoulder and smirked at the sight of him, Isaiah's hate sent shots through his body with his eyes.

He didn't give a fuck and just to show that nigga how much, after he ejaculated in her mouth, he yanked India's head back and told her to swallow.

India could not bear to be humiliated any longer, her pride made her refuse to be degraded any longer. Vigorously shaking her head no, praying that her pleading eyes would give this maniac a heart.

Of course, the urine seeped down her throat already, disgusting salty and bitter had insulted her taste buds. Of course, when he forcefully entered her mouth, the urine swished around her mouth. This was all disgusting but she did not want to volunteer to swallow his semen.

"No, no, Tango laughed. Okay, I'm not going to force you. She was relieved for a millisecond until he announced, "But, I will force your daughter.

Tango was an evil mother fucker and everyone in that house just got a glimpse of what this sick asshole was capable of by hearing the sounds of India's gags and gurgles as Tango pissed in her mouth.

"Bring the bitches downstairs!" He yelled to one of his men he sent to retrieve Isaiah's daughters from upstairs.

"No, I swallowed it. I swallowed it" she screamed at Tango! She sobbed quietly if she cried any louder she knew that she would throw him back up. And who knew how sadistic he would become if he saw that her body was rejecting him. India wanted to stick her fist down her throat and vomit. But she couldn't and she wouldn't. India wanted to kill herself, had she known her pride would have lead this monster to her child, she would have swallowed every drop of this inhumane asshole's bodily fluids.

"It's too late. You do what I say when I say it. Villarosa I see Now, let's see, um do I want the mother on dick duty, one daughter on salad duty and Isis. Ummm, I will enjoy eating that beautiful bitch's young pussy." He said foretelling his demented actions he will force the Villarosa women to perform.

"See what is taking so long?" he ordered

Coming back downstairs, the man came to whisper in his Boss's ear. "Isis, ain't' here!"

"Bring the other one down," Tango demanded

"Where is the beautiful Isis?" he questioned the mother as Mecca was pulled down the stairs by her long pigtails.

Mecca's 12-year-old body thumped down each step and each step intensified the pain she was feeling. India sobbed loudly and quickly gave a look at her husband.

"No, it's too late. Had Isis been here I would not have to subject your younger daughter to this lewd act. But, she's not so the punishment your husband has to face for disobeying me and making a fool out of me and my soldiers. Is by destroying his most prized possessions.

"Think of me as God, I will have mercy on your child and make her suck my dick," Tango said as he turned himself in the opposite direction.

"Daddy! Daddy please, the little girl screamed.

Isiah's face was plagued with guilt had he just given in or called somebody on the force to help with the harassment it wouldn't have come to this. His wife pleaded with him. But he could not, he was a man and would have been damned if some street thug was going to muscle him out of some money or his club.

The club and money seem so little compared to what he was losing now. Isiah shut his eyes tightly as if that alone would stop this torture of his family. That he could shut his baby girl's screams and his wife's sobs by such a simple act. Nothing would destroy this moment from his memory. How could he let it come to this he was too prideful to be a team player and he felt he was too invincible to go to authorities?

"Go ahead and suck that dick little Isis." He told Mecca and winked.

Mecca never watched any she had just turned twelve. She wasn't even curious about sex, she still played with dolls and had imaginary tea parties. And here she was staring at a penis a real penis. She shut her eyes tight with her lips just inches away from the head of this grown man's penis, she whispered, "Please dear God let me wake up out of this nightmare. Give my daddy superhero powers so he could bust out of those ropes and kill these men."

"What the fuck are you waiting for? My dick can't suck itself." Tango screamed slapping her in the mouth with his massive hard penis. "Isiah, man, Tango said moving away from Mecca's kneeling body. As she felt the evil move over her eyes popped open and a sigh of reliving came upon her. Tango walked over to Isiah un-shamefully that he was holding his dick in his hand for the whole room to see. "You mean to tell me you never taught your little bitches how to suck a dick?" He placed one hand on Isiah's shoulder still holding his dick with the other.

"How about daddy shows her how it's done?

Isiah turned his head with a sick look on his face.

Tango laughed, "If you don't suck it, then I will be forced to fuck your daughter in the ass, followed by several of my boys. How about we just run a train on mother and daughter? Daughter can get fucked in the ass and mom can suck the blood and feces off of it? That sounds like a plan doesn't it, Isiah?"

Once again with his dick in his hand Tango switches to the other side where Isiah turned his face and brought his penis up to his lips. Isiah turned the other way again. He was not going to suck another man's penis. He was not! What type of man would he be? How would people look at him in the neighborhood? How about his old colleagues on the force?

"Okay, I see you think you are more important than your child and your wife. Its okay for us to fuck your young ass daughter in the ass and make your wife suck shit off of our dicks, but you can't suck a clean penis? Mmmm, so if that doesn't move you, how about this-" he grabs the soldier holding Isiah at gunpoint, pistol from his waist. He then points it directly at India-I will shoot the bitch in the head if you don't suck my dick?" Isiah still didn't budge.

"No, Daddy, No! Mecca screamed as she ran over to her mother, intercepting the bullet that was meant for her, Mecca's body folded at the bottom of her mother's knees.

"NOOOOOOOOOO, you selfish motherfucker! My baby, India grabbed Mecca's body pressing her hand on the bullet wound to stop it from bleeding.

"Shut the fuck up!" Tango yelled.

"Your daughter got more heart than you. He turned towards Isiah, You see that shit 12 years old and she took one for the team. She took a bullet and you couldn't even suck a dick."

Isiah sobbed loudly, he knows he has failed his family. They untied him from the chair Isiah didn't try to lunge at Tango or his men, he just fell to his knees in grief.

Something in Isiah grasped a hold of his grief and turned into anger, and once Tango had his back turned away from Isiah, he snatched a pistol off of one of his goons, before he could pull the trigger, and they grabbed Isiah up by his throat.

"Oh, so we still haven't learned our lesson. You just can't get that pride of yours under control. Okay, grab that bitch and let's go." Tango said pointing to India.

The men picked India up kicking and screaming. She didn't care, she felt like dying as she watched her little girl bleed.

"You will get her back after I'm satisfied. I trust that you won't get the police involved; it wouldn't matter if you did. Since you have retired, some of your best men work for me."

Tango and his men left Isiah cradling his 12-year-old daughter, wondering what type of anguish his wife was going to endure. What type of torture his pride had left his family open for? A man's pride, what he won't stand for and what he will stand for can be seen as integrity. Being too prideful to ask for help from the very same men and women he reigned offer as Captain to protect his family is foolish.

Being too prideful in the streets when it comes to protecting your family and putting them first, even to preserve your own life, it will always be a sin even in the streets.

To Be Continued in the Novel Cold Thang by Ms. Pantha Jones

# The Lust-Up

# By

# Kieshawn Whaley

# **Chapter 1**

1 Corinthians 10: 5, 6 & 11

5: But with many of them God was not well pleased: for they were overthrown in the wilderness.
6: Now these things were our examples, to the intent we should not lust after evil things, as they also lusted.
11: Now all these things happened unto them for ensamples: and they are written for our admonition, upon whom the ends of the world are come.

"Put your arms through the bars," said the tired, overweight female correctional officer to the frightened fresh fish out of the water. She just felt depleted leaving from her psychological evolution. Her hands trembled. It felt as though her body was breaking down from the weight of this new world. The young lady placed her hands through the bars which allowed the correctional officer to remove the handcuffs. Damn, the officer thought as she remorsefully shook her head, why do they always end up this way?

The cold of the handcuffs was replaced by the reality that life as she knew it was now over. The new inmate closed her eyes and sighed, "I really fucked up now."

"Well you can at least introduce yourself, young lady," said an older woman who shared her cell.

"I'm sorry, I just..."

"I know sweetie. It's okay," she said. "My name is Thelma, but everyone in here calls me Mama T."

"Nice to meet you, Mama. My name is Lady. I mean Waukeshia, but my friends call me Lady."

"How long you down for?" Thelma asked.

Lady leaned back against the cell door bars and replied, "I don't know. I'm probably looking at least twenty-five years."

Mama T leaned back on her bed and said, "Damn. What the hell did a little thing like you do to be looking at that much time?"

"Let's just say Annalise Keating is the only one that can officially get away with murder," Lady said.

"How many?"

Still, in a world of disbelief at how she ended up here, Lady did not answer. She just held up one finger.

Mama T let out a laugh as she climbed down off of the top bunk. She walked up to Lady, looked her in the eyes and said, "Shit Lil girl. You only allegedly killed one person. Try killing your pimp and three of his other bitches. That's the crime that will get a bitch life three times over. But it is what it is. Might as well kick your feet up and settle in."

"You say that like prison is nothing," Lady said as she sat down on the bottom bunk.

"I wouldn't say that it's nothing. You just have to learn how to cope. You learn that all you can do is accept what happened and move on."

Lady closed her eyes rested the back of her head against the hard cell wall. Her mind begun to wander and replay the events that led her to this point in her life.

"Yes. Oh shit. Right there, daddy. Stay right there."

Lady's body quaked as Marcus' tongue sensually circled around her clitoris.

"Don't stop," Lady commanded as she pressed her

fingers even tighter to the back of his head, "I'm cumming. I'm fucking cumming? Oh my fucking god!"

Her body reached its climax, and Marcus buried his face deeper to bathe in all that she would give him.

"I love it when you cum all over my face like that," Marcus said as he slid over to wipe his face with the satin bed sheets.

Lady gathered herself off of the bed, looked back and smirked at how easy it was to please her lover. Marcus took care of her. He showered her with her every desire. Paid her bills and always kept money in her pocket. So pleasing him was all she wanted to do.

"Whatever it takes to make you happy baby," Lady said sweetly giving him a small peck on the cheek.

Lady looked around at the expensive hotel room as she started to get dressed. Buttoning up her white formal collar shirt and applying her medium length navy blue tie she imagined that she could live a life like this always. Instead of an expensive hotel room, they were making love a million dollar luxury home that she owned out in the country. A smile crept across Lady's face as she imagined being able to give her little brother Milo, the life that they both deserved as they played in seawater off the coast of Turks and Caicos. The real wealthy life where she could walk into a closet of Christian Louboutin's, Birkin bags and Alexander McQueen designer clothing. She imagined becoming the biggest mogul of her heart's desire and being posted on the cover of Forbes.

"What you thinking about, girl?" Marcus said as he looked himself over in the mirror as he got himself dressed.

"Oh nothing," Lady replied with a girlish smile on her face. "We got to hurry up though. Lunch has been over. I have to get back to class."

Marcus Lattimore was a topnotch lawyer with a few sexual fetishes that his wife would never even dream of doing. He particularly had a taste for young girls. In his mind, their tender barely touched bodies were as close to virgins as he was going to get. Marcus' wealth afforded him all of the luxurious toys that he could ever want. His little Lady was his most prized possession of them all. He felt no guilt when it came to his salacious affair. Lady was only doing a service for him. Nothing more, or nothing less.

"Marcus," Lady called to him as she impatiently checked the time on her phone, "I really need to get back to school."

"Chill babe, you've got plenty of time."

"No, I really don't. If I don't turn in this Spanish homework my teacher will drop my grade. I don't need that."

"You know baby, that's what I like about you. You stay on top of your shit. I promise you that when the time is right you won't have to worry about none of that anymore."

Marcus reached out and grabbed Lady's arm before she could make it to the hotel room door. He removed her book bag from her shoulder and let it drop to the floor. The soft sensual kiss to the neck made per panties wet once again.

Marcus placed his hands around her waist. Lady loved the sight that she saw in the mirror. She was so in love with Marcus that everything about him turned her on. A successful single lawyer who had fallen in love with a young seventeen-year-old girl from the projects. Giving her the promises that he would make her life better until they could both go public with each other. She would then become his wife, bare his children and reap the full benefits of being with him. Until then, they could be nothing more than friends with benefits.

"Alright, alright," he said. Reaching into his back pocket he pulled a stack of twenty dollar bills. Marcus peeled off five hundred dollars and handed it to her. "Go to the mall and buy something sexy for me."

"I got you, daddy," she replied.

Marcus kissed her on her lips once more before they headed out the door.

"Marcus."

"Yes."

"Do you really love me?"

Marcus pulled her close to him and answered, "Of course. Is that even a question?"

## Chapter 2

School had finally let out. Lady was running late out of the building. She had to run as fast as she could to catch the bus back to her home. When the bus arrived at the stop, Lady's head automatically dropped to the floor. The group of girls that hated and envied her the most stood in a circle smoking a blunt blocking her path.

"Well if it isn't Waukeshia Clarkston," Missy said with a snare in her nose.

Missy Franklin, head of the Misses Gang, hated the ground that Lady walked on. When Lady first got accepted into Baltimore City College's advanced program, Missy was the most heated that Lady didn't have to go to school with the other hood rats. She also hated the fact that Lady didn't kiss her ass like the rest on the block who was scared of her. Five foot seven, with a gorgeous honey colored, hourglass frame, Lady was everything that Missy was not.

"Girl, if your illegal ass don't leave me alone," Lady said snarling back at Missy and her gang. She wasn't scared of them and they didn't intimidate her. In her eyes, they were all talk. Turning the other way, she continued to move past the crowd.

"I want to know who you think you're talking to crack baby," Missy said laughing and passing the blunt to her homegirl.

Stopping dead in her tracks, Lady turned around and faced Missy and said, "I'm talking to you bitch. At least my daddy ain't no convicted rapist."

Missy clapped back, "Yeah, well at least my mama ain't out here sucking dick for a nick bags up and down the block hoe."

Lady stepped closer to Missy and answered, "My mom might suck dick, but at least my daddy didn't fuck my sister and suck my little brother's balls bitch."

Lady and Missy squared up and the other girls surrounded them. Lady knew that she was about to get jumped. Her only option was to fight her way out. Missy slapped Lady as hard as she could on the right side of her face. Lady barely flinched and returned fire with a left hand to Missy's chin. Her mouth clenched from the hit and she bit the side of her tongue. Blood started to trickle out of Missy's mouth. She was pissed because no other girl ever hit her back before.

The fight was on. Lady started firing punches directly at Missy's face and wouldn't stop swinging until she saw Missy hit the ground. Missy's best friend, Crystal, quickly tried to jump in but was snatched up by Rocko, a young gangster of the block and head of the 'G' crew. They ran the whole stick up from East to West Baltimore.

"Aye yo! Chill!" Rocko said breaking up the fight while laughing the whole time.

"Naw, let me at that bitch," Missy growled, snarling like a pit bull, her face bloody and bruised.

"I told you to stop fucking with me bitch!" Lady yelled as she grabbed her backpack from the ground. It had been stomped all over and the money that Marcus had given her earlier was showing out of the side of the bag. Rocko caught sight of money but didn't let it be known to anyone else.

"Go home, Missy! You wilding out right now," said Rocko, brushing her away and getting one of his boys to separate the girls.

"Come walk with me Lady," Rocko said smiling at her as he placed his arm around her shoulder. She looked over at Missy again and saw that she was safe to make her exit.

"You're still bad as shit yo," Rocko said as he looked over Lady's face.

"Rocko don't flirt with me," she said brushing his arm off of her shoulder irritated.

"Don't do me like that, Shor Shor. After I just saved your ass," he said as he grabbed her by the arm gently.

Lady rolled her eyes as noticed he was trying to use the common Baltimore term "Shor Shor" to try to get close to her. If a nigga from the block was into you, he would use the term to try to make you feel special. However, Lady was already onto Rocko's tricks.

"I'm serious Rocko. Leave me the fuck alone. I'm not your damn shor shor,"

Lady stormed in the direction of her building and

walked up the stairs leaving Rocko to stare at her ass every step of the way. Shaking his head, Rocko didn't really care about her brushing him off. He had plenty of females riding his dick. He was only concerned about the money that had been hanging outside of her book bag He knew that a seventeen-year-old girl from the hood with no job was either turning tricks or fucking with a nigga that had some money. Rocko already knew that Lady wasn't out here tricking like that, so it led him to one conclusion. He was going to figure out exactly who the nigga was and take him for everything he had.

"Yo, you gotta give that up man," said Rocko's friend, Yotti. "Lady ain't fucking with none of the niggas on the block Rock. Some other nigga got shorty head."

Rocko turned to Yotti and said, "Fuck Lady. I ain't even concerned with it. You ain't see the money she had. Shorty gotta nigga giving her the bag though. We gotta get it."

## Chapter 3

Marcus let out a loud moan of ecstasy as he came in Lady's mouth. Pulling up to her house was a first for Marcus. He never risked exposure by dropping Lady off in the hood but decided to take the risk today because she promised to suck the skin off of his dick in the car on the way.

"Shit babe, you're about to make me crash," he said as he slowly pulled the car over. His eyes rolled to the back of his head as she continued to perform on his dick until he went soft. You always get a nigga right." Marcus lifted Lady's head and buttoned up his pants.

"I always gotta get my baby right," she said wiping her mouth and popping in a piece of gum. "Thank you for picking me up tonight Marcus. I really needed to get away."

"You know I got you baby girl," he said as he put the car back in drive. I'll see you later." Marcus whipped his black Mercedes off the curb and sped off before Lady was barely out of the car. She stood and watched his taillights disappear before she walked to her building.

Lady walked up the steps and swiftly moved past the dope boys that stayed posted in her hallway. With a man like Marcus, they were not worth her time.

"I see you shor," Rocko said coming out of a hidden corner. He had watched her get out of the Benz and enter into the hallway. In fact, he had been watching Lady's and tracking her whereabouts for the last two weeks. She pulled out her house key and rolled her eyes at Rocko. Giving a slight chuckle, he now had verified proof that Lady was fucking with a rich nigga and that he had to hit a lick. Putting his mastermind to work, he now had the perfect plan on how he was going to get what he wanted.

The house smelled of rotten liquor, stale cigarettes, and marijuana. The smoke smacked Lady in the face as soon as she entered. Lady looked at her mother swaying with a 4Loko in her hand with disgust. Her mother and her drug buddies had old school music playing and were singing along to Marvin Gaye while they were getting fucked up.

"Hey baby," she slurred. "Come give your mama some

sugar."

"Nah, I'm good yo," Lady said while moving to pick up her two-year-old little brother, Milo, from the living room floor. "I can't believe you have Milo out here in all this smoke."

Lady buried Milo's in her chest and walked swiftly to her bedroom and locked the door behind her. A single tear flowed down her cheek as she fixed the sheets on her mattress. This wasn't what her mother was supposed to be like. Her mother wasn't supposed to be on drugs or an alcoholic. She was supposed to be a successful nurse helping to make people better like she always dreamed of. It wasn't until Lady's mother suffered a terrible back injury at the time that the drugs and alcohol took control of her life. She had Milo by accident a couple of years ago with another user which made her condition worse. Lady found it ironic how her mother's dream was the direct opposite of her life-long goal.

Lady hated the way they lived. Sleeping on old mattresses on the floor, roaches that crawled up the walls every night. Her little brother was two years old and still sleeping in a damn crib. They even had to share a room. Everything was on Lady. She was the one that tried to keep everything together. She took care of Milo, paid for everything and hid her money in different hiding spots away from her dope fiend mother. All in all, she was the mother of the family.

"Come on Milo, let's lay down baby," she said picking him up and cuddling him in her bed. Closing her eyes, tears of sadness flowed more often than happiness. She wanted out and that is why Marcus was so important to her. The small moments they shared together where he made love to her and treated her like a queen meant everything to her. On top of taking care of her with the money, his contributions put tiny bandages on the large wounds that her mother has caused. She couldn't wait until the day she was of age so that she could finally go public with him and reap the benefits of his wealthy life. The thought of this lightened her heart and she smiled. She would finally be in a situation where she had money. In her neighborhood, if you had money then all of your issues were solved. Marcus

was her savior and she would love him. Truthfully, Lady

would love his money even more. Watching Milo dose off to

sleep, she knew they were going to be okay. Marcus, her

and Milo were going to have their own family and live the

perfect life.


Lady woke up the next morning to Milo with an old

pacifier in his mouth and playing with an empty box on the

floor. Her heart instantly went into a panic as she noticed

that her classic Usher poster had been ripped and was

hanging from the wall. She had put her stash in the box

and hid it in the hole in the wall behind the poster.

Immediately, she jumped up and ran into the living room

only to find her mother gone with the door slightly cracked.

Lady was steaming hot. The five thousand dollars

that she had saved were gone and there was nothing that

she could do about it. Milo sat clueless to the chaos as he

played with the box and sucked on his pacifier. If it was not for him, Lady would have killed her mother a long time ago. She looked down at Milo she knew she had to be the one to set the example. He sat a child without a care in the world and she wished that she could turn back the hands of time and chose her own family. Through all the bullshit she had to deal with no one knew just how defeated she felt at this moment. Lady picked up her phone and dialed Marcus' number. He worked a crazy schedule and often didn't respond to her until he was free

A few hours later Lady's mother came stumbling through the door. Her clothes smelled of old liquor and like she had been outside roaming the streets for hours. Lady couldn't wait for her to come through the door so she could confront her. Shaking her head, she immediately stood up and faced her mother.

"Where is my money bitch?" asked Lady.

Before her mother could respond to the question she vomited all over the dirty floor.

"You nasty bitch. Where's my fucking money!"

"Baby... baby they robbed me," she said as she hit the

living room floor. Vengeance filled Lady as she began to swing on her mother with the thick studded belt she had in hand.

"You have the nerve to steal from me when I provide for us!" she yelled and eventually the swinging of the belt turned into her swinging with her fist.

Her mother had already been attacked but Lady planned to do far worse than what the person who robbed her did. Trying to fight her off her mother was too weak to move. Lady began to punch her in the stomach she vomited on the floor once again.

"You trifling thieving bitch! Clean yourself up this time!" Lady said. "As a matter of fact, get the fuck out my house!"

"I have no other place to go!" pleaded her mother. "Lady please don't do this. I'll do better I promise."

Lady grabbed her mother by her raggedy ponytail and dragged her down the hallway. "Get outta here Marjorie and don't come back until you get some fucking help!"

Lady hated to throw her mother out because she

knew she didn't have anyone else. There was no other choice. She needed peace and sanity because she was tired. Tired of someone stealing from her and neglecting her little brother. Most of all Lady was tired of her not giving either one of them the love a mother was supposed to give.

Lady walked into her room and was glad that Milo was still sound asleep. She also needed time to grieve because kicking her mother out was like experiencing a death. She had never known how it felt to feel the love of a father or mother because they both had abandoned her emotionally and physically. Looking down at Milo the release she hoped for flowed and she promised that she would never put him through what their mother had. She leaned over, kissed him on his forehead and whispered, "I love you."

Lady had dropped Milo off at the neighbor's house in the evening so that she could have some time to clear her head. She was thankful for her neighbor, Misty, who was like the neighborhood mom to all the lost girls. She had heard all the commotion and came over to help her clean up the mess her mother made. Walking outside of the building and down the block, the fresh air made Lady feel like she could breathe again. She walked a few blocks over from her house and eventually she ran into a girl from her block named Shawnee.

"Hey girl, what's up?" Shawnee as she walked up to Lady

"Nothing girl, just out trying to clear my head a little you know," Lady said. "What are you doing out here so late?"

"I'm just kicking it. It ain't shit to do in the house," Shawnee said. "I think I got something you need though. Do you want to hit this blunt with me? I'm lonely tonight, and I don't want to smoke by myself."

Lady thought about it for a second then said, "Fuck it. You only live once right?"

"Aye, let's slide to this little alley though. The boys been out here ya heard?" Shawnee said as she motioned towards the entrance to the alley.

"Cool," Lady said approaching the alley with

Shawnee. It was dark but Shawnee shined a little light that leads the way right to the middle.

"We good girl," said Shawnee as she stopped short towards the middle of the alley.

Shawnee sparked the blunt and hit it a couple times before she passed it to Lady. Lady took a few pulls from the blunt, and her world instantly became cloudy.

"I don't know what that shit is, but I'm good," Lady said her words slurring a bit.

"Yo, you good ma?" Shawnee asked with a little laugh. Lady felt a bit woozy, but she knew she had to keep her composure in front of Shawnee. All of sudden, the little light that shined went completely black and Lady couldn't see a thing.

"Yo, shine the light," Lady said but Shawnee didn't say a word. The footsteps that approached her were quick and being in the dark made Lady feel uneasy. No sooner than she put her hands up to defend whoever was coming after her, Lady felt a bag roughly go over her head. Lady tried to fight back, but her arms and legs were being restrained. It then became painfully clear that Shawnee had set her up.

"Put that bitch in the trunk!" ordered one of the voices in the darkness.

Lady tried to cry out, but the sound of the trunk slamming shut reduced her to scared silence. Her life was now in their hands.

## Chapter 4

"Good morning Shor Shor," Rocko said as he pulled the bag from over Lady's head. She sat in a shitty motel room tied to a chair. Lady opened her eyes and saw that Rocko was in the room with Shawnee and Yotti. Lady scowled at Shawnee as she wanted to square her up with right then and there. However, she knew what position she was sitting in, so she just mean mugged her from across the room.

"What the fuck Rock!" Lady yelled out in anger. "You used that dirty bitch to set me up? "That's some bitch ass nigga shit."

Without saying a word, Rocko bloodied her nose with a devastating slap across the face. Rocko turned the chair so that Lady was seated facing the bed. He sat down in front of her and started to speak.

"I only have a few questions and depending on how you answer you might make it out of this shit alive. So listen carefully because a nigga don't like to repeat himself. Do I make myself clear?

Lady slowly nodded her head.

"So, my mans right here already got the stash your moms had. That got me to  thinking though." Rocko started to stroke the hairs on his beard before he continued, "If a crackhead can get a hold of some stacks from her fine ass daughter, then I know we can get more? So I watched you. I saw that old ass nigga you were with, in the Benz. That is your n=old as nigga right?"

"Yeah...yes," Lady stuttered.

"Good answer. Rocko leaned in closer and asked, "Where can we find him?

"Um...Annapolis," Lady answered nervously.

"You don't sound too sure ma," Rocko said removing his weapon from the holster.

"I'm sure! I'm sure!"

Rocko leaned in even closer to Lady so that his ear rested against her lips. "What's the address?

Lady said it low enough so that only Rocko could hear. Satisfied, Rocko untied Lady and handed her the cell phone that they confiscated before stuffing her in the trunk.

"Dial that nigga's number and set this shit up. You better hope that he answers. Your life depends on it."

Lady's hands trembled as she searched through her contacts to find Marcus' name. She pressed on his name and hit send while she said a silent prayer for him to answer. After the fourth ring, a clearly agitated Marcus answered.

"Why the hell are you calling me right now? You know what I said.

"Marcus, please don't be mad. I need you," she cried, the tears streaming down her face.

"Can it wait? I have a lot of work to do and it's late."

A visibly irritated Rocko snatched the phone from Lady and spoke directly to Marcus.

"Yo nigga, we got your bitch over here and I'm about to pop shorty head clean off if you don't give a nigga what he wants."

Marcus started to laugh. "My bitch? Is this

some kind of joke? Who is this?"

This angered Rocko. He placed his hand around lady's throat and started to squeeze. Lady pleaded for him to stop.

"Now nigga, does this sound like I'm muthafucking joking?"

The phone got quiet on Marcus's end. He could hear the sound of her choking and gasping for air. He gathered himself and quietly asked, "What is it that you want?"

"I want fifty k or this bitch is dead."

"Fifty thousand dollars! Nigga are you crazy? Where the fuck am I going to get fifty thousand dollars? Go ahead and do whatever you got to do?"

"What?" Rocko said almost in a state of shock.

"I said do whatever you got to do. Listen, son, I have a wife and kids. Ain't no pussy from no little high school hoe worth me losing my family. I can't risk my career and freedom. She got herself into it, and I will give you one hundred k to get me out of it."

Lady broke down to the point that she was almost hysterical. After the months that they had spent together and the love that they had created she was devastated that it was all a lie. At that moment she no longer cared whether she lived or died.

"A'ight my nigga. You got it," Rocko said as he pulled the trigger.

The sound of the gunshot caused Marcus dropped the phone. Then there was silence.

"Damn!" Rocko exclaimed, "I can't believe that that nigga really said kill her and he will give me a hunnit racks. That's a cold muthafucka."

Lady looked up with tears in her eyes and asked, "Rocko, are you really going to kill me? Think about Milo. If you kill me, there will be no one else left to love him in this world. I am all that he has."

Never in his life has Rocko hesitated to pull the trigger. He was a real a soldier that has ever walked the streets of Baltimore. This time, however, was different. He had a code. Never catch a body that doesn't deserve to be caught. He put the gun down and said, "Nah, Shor Shor, I ain't gonna kill you. You had enough."

Lady closed her eyes and exhaled. "Thank you, Rocko."

"Don't thank me. Shit was just fucked up how that nigga just left you for dead."

"Well fuck him now!" Vengeance now took over Lady's heart. She looked deep into Rocco's eyes and said, "If you still want to get that money, then let's go get it."


Rocko laughed, "Let's? This ain't no let's, and this ain't no we. This ain't the life for you Lady.

"No...fuck that. If you want the money, I was a piece of the pie, or you might as well just kill me."

"Yo let me at this bitch," Shawnee said as she tried to approach.

"Shawnee you need to chill. Now ain't the fucking time."

Lady told Rocko to Shawnee go. Rocko stepped back and lunged for Shawnee, knocking her to the ground.

Lady landed on top of Shawnee began to throw hard punches to her face. She was giving Shawnee the ass whooping that she deserved. After a few seconds, Rocko told Yotti to bark it up.

"Y'all done now?" he chuckled.

"Now that I got that off my chest we can talk," Lady said never taking her eyes off of Shawnee. "I have a plan but you have to promise not to hurt me or Milo"

Shaking his head, Rocko gave his non-verbal agreement to Lady's condition.

"A'ight so here's what we need to do."

Lady and the crew went over the plan with precise detail and instruction. She knew that she could no longer be that love struck little girl who fell for the older man. Her salvation was gone. She had to be cold and calculating to make sure that she survived and could make a way for Milo and herself to get away. Above all else, Lady knew that Marcus had to pay.

## Chapter 5

"Oh yes, daddy... fuck me just like that," Shawnee screamed as Marcus plowed deeper inside of her. Positioned across the bed on his stomach, Shawnee pretended to enjoy the sexual acts that were being performed on her. If she had it her way, another bitch would be laying in this position and getting fucked in the ass over and over again. She hated herself for it, but the promise of the money made her go all in for the job. It was what she had to do.

Nearing the point of release, Marcus moaned as he pulled out and came all over Shawnee's ass. Thankful that it was finally over, Shawnee rolled her eyes Shawnee then rolled over onto her back before flashing a fake smile. Marcus collapsed in a state of bliss right down next to her.

Shawnee had taken Lady's place for a good two weeks. Eager to put the memory of Lady out of his mind, Marcus quickly accepted her. So much so that she was able to make it to his house.

"Damn girl," Marcus said, barely able to catch his

breath. 'that thick chocolate ass is fire."

"Am I better than your other bitches?"

"Baby, you are the best that I have ever had."

"That makes me happy. I'll be right back. I have to use the bathroom."

Marcus grabbed his dick with both hands and said, "Hurry back. I need some more of that."

Shawnee was happy that all of this was finally about to be over. She made her way to the bathroom and called Lady to let her know that the side door was open.

"You alright in there?" Marcus called as he began to stroke himself.

"Here I come baby," she said. "You remember that surprise I told you I have for you?"

"Yeah what's that?" Marcus asked.

"I was thinking about bringing in another girl and she's here," Shawnee said with a smile. Even though Marcus wasn't pleased with the fact that Shawnee had given someone his address, he was more excited about the thought of a threesome.

"Go get her," Marcus said excited and he held the smile on his face until he saw Lady walk in with two guns pointed at his head.

As Lady got closer, she handed one of the guns to Shawnee. Her heart was cold as ice with an expression on her face to match. She couldn't stand the sight of Marcus, sitting there with a hard dick having just lain up with Shawnee. She was already upset but this made her pipes steaming hot.

Shock mixed with the feeling of betrayal, Marcus sat up in the bed and yelled at Shawnee, "Bitch you set me up!"

Shawnee smiled and said, "Don't take it, personal baby. It was just business. Now, why don't you tell us what the combination to the safe is love."

"Fuck you, bitch! I ain't telling you shit."

"Oh, you're so disrespectful." Shawnee turned the gun around and smacked Marcus across the face. "The next time you disrespect me, I'm putting a bullet in your face.

Marcus turned his attention to Lady. He tried to appeal to the love that she once felt for him. "Lady..."

Lady quickly cut him off. "Shut up! I don't want to hear any more of your lies nigga! Shut the fuck up and tell us the combo to the safe. What is the fucking combination!"

The anger inside of her caused Lady to lose control. She raised the gun high over her head and brought it crashing down on Marcus' temple.

"Oh shit!" said a shocked Shawnee. "Lady, look at what the fuck you did!"

The force of the blow almost caused Marcus to pass out. Now fearing for his life, he gave them the combination.

"I'm going to get the money," Shawnee said and quickly ran out of the room.

Lady kept the gun trained on Marcus' face. Being back inside of the room caused a tidal wave of emotion to overcome her. The love that she still had for him would never go away. She so desperately wanted all of this to be a dream.

"Lady, you don't have to do this. I love you. I have always loved you. I was just scared to break up my family."

Lady took a few steps back and lowered her gun. "Don't Marcus. Don't you dare? What about my family? You were supposed to be my way out. You were supposed to be Milo's way out. You ruined that."

"We can still..."

Lady fired a shot into Marcus' leg.

"Say one more word and I will kill you."

Suddenly, the sound of tired screeching could be heard outside. Lady quickly ran to the bedroom window to see what was going on. To her horror, she saw Shawnee and Rocko speeding away.

"Did you get the money?" asked Rocko impatiently waiting for the answer.

"Yeah. I took all of it."

"That's my bitch!" Rocko pulled out a burner phone and dialed the police. When they answered, he told them that he heard gunfire at the residence.

As she watched the car speed away, Lady knew that there was no way out for her. No, her life was over. She walked over towards Marcus and sat down on the bed next to him. Her eyes were cold and lifeless as they looked around the room at all of the pictures of Marcus and his family. She had never seen them, or maybe she was just so blinded by her lust for his money and a better life that she chose to ignore the fact that they were there.

Lady lay down and placed her head on Marcus' lap. She could hear the sirens off in the distance. She positioned her head so that she was staring up at him. With tears in her eyes, she asked, "Marcus, did you ever really love me? Was it true when you said that you wanted to be the only man in my life?

Marcus heard the sirens too. He knew that all he had to do was play on Lady's naivety a few minutes longer and he would survive. Marcus weakly muttered, "Yes, Lady, I was telling the truth. Please forgive me. I don't want to live without you."

Lady smiled one last time. She sat up to kiss Marcus, closed her eyes and said, "Don't worry baby. You won't have to."

Lady pulled the trigger and the shot ended Marcus'

life instantly. She then laid her head on his chest and waited for the police to come and take her away.

**

"So... that's how I ended up here," Lady said.

"It's amazing what a young girl in lust will do... but word of advice. These niggas are just not worth it," Thelma said.

"Lust, I loved that nigga."

"Naw, Baby Girl that was lust. Read the definitions; compare them to what got you in here. And I betcha it's more lust than love."

"You might be right. When it came down to it, it wasn't about the love or lust anymore. Hell... when I think about it I don't even know what love really is. It was about the pain and making him feel what I felt.... I let my own vengeance get the best of me," Lady said reflecting.

"I'll tell you like my mother told me... it's a thin line between love and hate," Thelma said. "Now, let me tell you about some real gangsta shit that happened back in my day. See my pimp's name was-"

Lady couldn't help but laugh at Thelma and knew off the bat that she would have a friend in her as long as she did her bid. Listening to Thelma she tuned her out for a second as she thought about Marcus. Who did she think she was to play God and take his life away? If the boys hadn't have gotten to her she was definitely was going to pull the trigger on herself next. She wished she would have done the latter or she wouldn't be in this situation. She questioned God why she ended up in this life of having a horrible mother, making the decision to leave Milo and ending up in prison.

The consequences of her decisions leaving her brother motherless, in foster care and her having no one to support her. Her answer was brought to her mind quickly as she realized that she committed one of the seven deadly sins: Lust. She and Marcus both fell to the stronghold of lust he lusted after young girls committing adultery and although she loved Marcus she knew she was lusting after his money. Would she have cared if

Marcus would have told her he was married? She didn't

know and she will never have to find out.

# Gluttony of Spirits

## By

## Tiara Bland

## Chapter 1

Spirits
strong distilled liquor such as brandy, whiskey, gin, or rum.
synonyms: strong liquor/drink;
        hard stuff, firewater, hooch
        "he drinks spirits"
a volatile liquid, especially a fuel, prepared by distillation.

"911, What is your emergency?" the operator said.

Kim could barely utter the word help into her

cellphone but she managed to in a whisper, "Help!"

"Ma'am, are you saying help?" the operator said

urgently into the phone.

"Help, she whispered into the phone stronger than

before. She felt her self-struggling to keep her eyes open.

The room was spinning her vision went blurry as she tried

to focus on her husband's dead body on the floor. As she

lost consciousness the memories of their relationship

flooded her mind.

Tyrone Evans grew up in Gary, Indiana with his mother Towanda as his guide. She was a holy woman so Tyrone grew up in the church. They attended Zion Progressive on 13th and Connecticut. His father left when he was two years old. His family did not come from much so he always had dreams of getting out of the hood and giving his mother the life she deserved. He graduated from Roosevelt High School, got accepted to Harvard and then to Harvard Law school.

Tyrone strived to be wealthy by the time he hit the age of 25, become Partner of his firm before thirty. He wanted to have his own practice by the time he was thirty-two. He was all about representing where he came from but he felt as if he was not going to be able to achieve all of his goals living in Gary. He tried to talk his mother into moving out of Gary and living with him. His mother always told him, with everything that his father put her through. She deserved to own that house and enjoy it alone. So, he made the trip from Maryland to Indiana every 6 months to visit her. Who knew on his latest visit, he would meet the woman who would change his life?

Kimberly Watson was born in Houston, Texas. She was 5'4 with hazel eyes, slim waist, hourglass figure and southern bell charm along with accent kept plenty of men coming her way. Kim had a lot of things going on for her but on the inside, she was a lost soul and insecure about herself.

Kim grew up watching her mom who was just as beautiful as she, degrade herself just so they can have food to eat and clothes on their backs. Running after men, getting beat and used by men who never wanted her for more than sex. She never really knew what to expect from the men her mom brought home.

The men started looking her with the same lust in their eyes' as they had for her mother. It was so unbearable, she ran away to Gary when she was sixteen years old. Leaving her mother to focus on whatever man she was taking care of that month. But she took something with her that she should have left with her mom. Her low-self-esteem and insecurities of being unworthy

Since she got there, all she experienced was pain and bad luck.

Kim was never one to be social with everyone she met. She picked and chose who she let into her heart. Unfortunately for her, it was all the wrong people. She got involved with men who used drugs or finessed her into sex trafficking ring sex just to please the men who said they would "take care of her or loved her" just to keep a man in her life and a place to lay her head. The world was a cold and cruel place in her eyes, and there was no one who could tell her different.

After going from place to place and toxic men who would not commit to her for the last seven years, Kim decided to try to change her life, and get away from all the pain she endured. She went to the place she thought she could get the help she needed but wanted so desperately Church. She decided to see if there was really a God and if He still knew she existed in the world. She had a feeling he gave up on her because of the things she did. She sat quietly in the back and listened to the pastor preach. It felt like he was talking directly to her.

It was as if he knew her life story. When the altar call came, she rose to her feet and as she made her way to the altar she could feel the eyes on her. She kept going until finally she was in the front and she decided to dedicate her life to the lord. It was at the altar that she met Tyrone. He was in town for a visit and when he came, he always helped at the church. He was bringing someone to the altar and he laid eyes on her. There she was, this beautiful creature who looked as if she had so much hurt in her heart and still found time to give her life to God. He knew then and there he had to get to know her and change her life. Plus, she seemed desperate for love.

When the pastor finished his prayer and he told them how they just made the most important decision of their lives, she felt a huge burden lift from her shoulders. For the first time in a long time, she smiled. She just knew everything was going to turn around in her life. When she went back to her seat, he was standing there. As she made her way down the row, she realized that he was following her, and when she sat down he sat down beside her. Church was almost over so he knew he wouldn't have to wait very long to get to know the woman beside him.

When the church was over, Tyrone was full of confidence as he approached Kim. He approached like a gentleman and said: "Excuse me miss, but I cannot seem to take my eyes off of you."

Kim blushed because he was so handsome and from the looks of him, he had a lot of money and that was all she wanted. She replied with a handshake and introduction: "Well since you can't take them from me, why haven't you asked my name?"

He laughed, "What is your name?

"Kimberly but you can call me Kim," she replied reaching out her hand.

Tyrone smiled, took her hand and kissed it, "I would love to take you to dinner."

Kim returned his smile, "I would love to have dinner

with you.

Tyrone picked Kim up at 8 pm that night and to her surprise, he took on a ride to his private jet where he whisked her to one of the best restaurants in New York. He wined and dined her.

During dinner, he asked her question that she was reluctant to answer. It was then that he learned of her past and when he told her he understood and that she was safe with him, she felt at ease with knowing it was something different about this man. But not once did Tyrone talk about himself.

After six months of dating and becoming comfortable with each other, Tyrone finally asked Kim to carry on his last name. With thoughts of all her problems ending with this man, Kim accepted. She didn't feel rushed because she was in love and she felt he was a present from God because of how they met.

Six months later Kim and Tyrone were married at a private ceremony at a beach in Miami. Kim had no one to invite since she had not talked to her mother since she ran away. Her maid of honor was Tyrone's mother, Mrs. Evans. She wore a beautiful long gown and the glow illuminating her face showed how happy she really was to be marrying this man. Tyrone was equally excited as he watched her walk down the aisle. To have this beautiful bride and to know she would be his for the rest of their lives warmed his heart.

They honeymooned in the Bahamas and had a lot of good memories. Waiting to make love until marriage was something Kim wasn't used to, but she honored Tyrone even more. Kim could not wait to start her new life with her husband. She felt it was the best decision she ever made in her life. Tyrone was everything she needed in a man: Christian, wealthy and loving. She couldn't have asked for anything or anyone better. They stayed on their honeymoon for two weeks and when they returned home it was like they never left their honeymoon.  Kim was enthused that everything was turning out for the best. She had it all and most importantly she had Tyrone to share it with her.

Their house was huge with four bathrooms, seven bedrooms, living room, office, den, dining room, laundry room and complete basement with bar and weight room. Not to mention the two cars parked in the driveway and the other two in the garage. She felt proud that she finally found someone who was God-fearing, in church, wealthy and treated her like a queen. This was a fairytale, she felt undeserving of this man, of this lifestyle he was giving her, she promised herself she would do anything and everything to protect her life as Mrs. Tyrone Evans.

Kim still asked, "Husband, I know you are a Lawyer and Lawyers are well off, but this she said in awe as she turned around in circles with her arms spread. Exactly, what type of lawyer are you?" "I'm a partner at Evans, Briggs, and Moore law firm, we deal in criminal law. but I bought this house when you said yes to marrying me," he replied with a chuckle.

She laughed and said, "I always thought partners' at Law firms were old men, you must bring them in a lot of money and wins."

"Yes I do, but let's not talk about that now, and let's have a toast." He offered her a glass of champagne and she drank it. That night as Kim lay securely in her husband arms, she thanked God for her husband and silently cried tears of joy.

## Chapter 2

The first five years were wonderful for Kim. She never had to work because Tyrone made her feel like the queen she deserved to be. Her husband not only did for her but he catered to her every need and want. They went to church together and he helped her become saved. He got her into reading the bible and how to understand it. The only expectation he required of her was to be there for him when he returned from a long, tedious day at work. Of course, she had no choice but to make the man of her dreams happy. He always came home with jewelry, flowers, or any romantic surprise he could think of. She felt truly blessed and nothing could change that feeling in her eyes.

It was their sixth anniversary, Kim decided to surprise her husband with a romantic dinner that night and she had another surprise. She cooked all his favorite foods: Steak, baked potatoes, greens, cornbread, and for dessert her famous chocolate cake with vanilla filling. She ran his bath water, lit candles and put rose petals everywhere around the room. She had soft R&B playing from the radio.

She put on her sexiest outfit and waited for her King to arrive. She had a wonderful and exciting secret she just couldn't wait to tell him.

At 10 pm when Tyrone didn't show, she blew out what was left as a candle and called him. When he answered she said, "Baby where are you? It's our anniversary?"

"I'm still at the office, I got a new case today and I need to catch up on it."

Disappointed that he hadn't called to tell her this news or warn her beforehand that he might have to be at the office late on their anniversary she put on a fake understanding voice, "That's ok we can always celebrate on the weekend."

Part of her had hoped that would guilt him into coming home but all she got was, "That sounds like a good idea, I will see you later baby. Don't wait up." and hung up without so much as a happy anniversary or I love you.

She was hurt but she knew he would eventually come

home. She put the food up and but her matching silk red rob on. She fell asleep waiting for her husband while she listened to music through her headphones.

An hour had passed but she was awakened by the urge to be pleasured and he still wasn't home yet. It didn't seem as if her husband was going to come to please her on their anniversary. It was going on 12 o'clock in the morning and Kim was going at it.

Tyrone came in the house like a chaotic tornado and he was yelling drunkenly through the house. Being unaware of his presence she was lost in the movement of her hands and the music serenading her ears. He came into the bedroom, pausing at the sight of his wife pleasing herself. Disgusted and feeling less than a man, Tyrone approached her quickly as she lay in their bed, thinking about God knows who, while she played with herself. He snatched the headphones out of her ears and out of her iPod.

Startled, Kim sat up in bed to see the look of disgust on her husband's face, like he had caught her cheating with another man. She couldn't understand why he was so upset; she thought any man would have seen what she was doing as sexy foreplay, so why was he so upset?

"What seems to be troubling you?" Kim said in a playful tone.

Tyrone drew his fist back ready to punch her but he opts just to smack the taste out her mouth. Kim's head flew sideways, instantly she was caught off guard. She could tell he was drunk and she tried to get him to calm down, but he stormed out of the room. Kim followed him around the house as Tyrone seemed to be searching for something. On his heels, she repeatedly asked him, "What did I do wrong?"

When he finally made it to his home office, he pulled out a thick yardstick. Not knowing what was going on she came up behind him and touched his arm and it was as if something had taken over him. He grabbed her by her right hand and roughly pulled her down to her knees.

"Was this the hand you were touching my body with, the hole I enter and my children will exit out of?" he grabbed her face and yelled, "Is this the hand! She was stunned by the question and this side of him, so all she could do was nod her head yes. He dragged her by the hand he felt she defiled their marital bed with, towards the middle of his office where his bibles were.

He had two The King James Version and The New International Version, sitting on a Mahogany double podium, "Kneel before God's words and don't move, he said as he stood behind the podium and opened both bibles.

As if he was prosecuting someone in the courtroom his voice boomed with accusations, "Marriage should be honored by all, and the marriage bed kept pure, for God will judge the adulterer and the sexually immoral. Hebrews 13:4, New International Version."

"Let's go to the King James Version, he executed every word like he was in the courtroom, "Marriage is honorable in all, and the bed undefiled" but whoremongers and adulterers God will judge. (Hebrews 13:4) See no matter what version you read it all boils down to you defiling our marital bed.

You're an adulterer and a whoremonger. Who were you thinking about as you touch what is mine?" He questioned as he walked towards her with the thick yardstick.

Still, in devastation and in horrific awe of this stranger she married, she stuttered scared of what he was capable of," Y-Y-You, she pleaded as she was still on her knees. In her head she wondered why she was still on her knees, being reprimanded like a child.

"Your facial expressions have never displayed so much euphoria when I make you climax. So I don't believe you were thinking about me. Were you lusting after one of those heathens you used to date? Don't answer that question, just hold still, he said as he raised the yardstick and with force hit her hand several times.

After her initial shock wore off, she grabbed the stick in midair she was filled with anger but dared not strike her husband back, that wasn't the biblical way. That set him off because he started to punch her and kick her. The punches and the kicks made her try to fight back but the alcohol made Tyrone stronger. When she finally yelled "Lord Jesus, please make him stop hurting me", Tyrone finally realized what he was doing. He froze but he tried to justify his actions with a bible scripture he quoted Timothy 2:11-15 and left out the room. Surprisingly, after the plethora of drinks, he downed he gave a soberly magnificent performance but was still drunk as he stumbled upstairs to their Master Bedroom. It seemed no matter what state of mind he was in when it came to scripture he knew it.

Kim ran to the bathroom in his office and when she saw her face she cried so hard she was shaking as she looked down her hand was red and swollen. She didn't know what had come over him to make him hurt her like this. He was not the man she married, "God, Who is this beast of a man? What demon has possessed my husband, Lord? Please Dear God, tell me what to do." She pleaded as she washed her face the best way she could. She believed now that she was saved, God would never let one of his children go through this.

Hours passed and Tyrone came back downstairs to

find his wife curled up in front of the fireplace asleep with tears of pain dried up on her cheeks. He picked her up and as he saw her face, he felt remorse for his actions because of the damage he did to her beautiful face. Next time he reasoned I will beat her lower into submission just not in her face.

Kim felt him pick her up but she dare not give away that she was awake. He placed her gently down on the bed he tore her sexy outfit off and put her in a long white nightgown that he felt suited for the wife of a church-going man. He kissed her lips and got on his knees to pray as he always did throughout the day. He finally lay next to his wife and went to sleep.

His wife, however, let her tears bring her to slumber after she prayed that the beast in her husband would return from whence it came from. But, if someone shows you who they are, believe them.

After finally falling asleep at six in the morning, she was awakened by the sound of doors slamming and her husband talking to someone. She didn't know how to approach him after what he did to her. She got out the bed and looked at the clock. It was nine in the morning and she had a horrible headache. She slowly walked to the door to hear who he was talking to, but she couldn't hear him too well. So she walked downstairs to his office and she overheard him say, "You'll be sorry you fired me. I can assure you of that."

She knocked on the door and when she opened it, he rushed off the phone, "I'll call you later" and hung up.

"Would you like some breakfast honey?" Kim asked, he looked at her face and a wave of guilt surfaced.

"No thank you, Baby." He replied

She started to walk out of the room when he grabbed her by her arm. She flinched, he tried to ignore it but part of him was proud of the way she flinched, "I am so sorry for what I did to your face. I hope you find it in your heart to forgive me. I just have been so stressed and yesterday I lost my job due to some foolishness that I had nothing to do with. I had a few drinks to deal with it and I just snapped. I had no right to take it out on you

"That's alright. This is a pretty stressful thing for you to deal with. I just want you to talk to me next time. I am here for you no matter what because I am your wife. Drinking will not make it go away. Are you going to be okay?" She asked playing right into his game to break her into complete submission.

"I'll be fine. I'm a wanted lawyer so I can have a job in no time and could even start my own practice." He kissed her and told her "I'll never do it again if you don't ever do that again. I love you so much, that the thought of the possibility of you just thinking of another man", He shook his head and didn't finish his sentence as if what he was about to say was too calamitous to say.

He started to let tears run down his face deliberately, as he ran his hand across the damage he had done to her face, "I will never do this to you again, he told her. Kim saw the tears and the sincerity in his eyes and she cried. She accepted his I'm sorry kisses as he kissed her face. She hoped he meant it and she wanted to believe him but her past was trying to seep into her mind and remind her of her

mother's life, "that it only gets worse after the first time. But

God was on her side? Now, that she was one of his

children? She never heard her mom talk about God. They

never went to church. Why is the same thing happening to

her? Maybe this was one of God's tests? A test of her faith?

A test of submission to her husband?

## Chapter 3

### Several days later

After cooking breakfast and Tyrone blessed the food, he cleared his throat "I need you to be ready by 12, we're going to a picnic with some of my colleagues and their wives."

Quickly her eyes widen and she immediately touched her face but hurriedly put her hand back down, "What do I need to prepare?" she asked meekly. She was hoping her bruises faded enough for her to use foundation to clean it up.

"Bring beverages, he said as he got up to go get ready.

She didn't know how she was going to cover her face but she did it the best way she could. She got three bottles of Mascoto, two bottles of champagne, bottled water and juice. When Tyrone offered her a glass of her favorite wine (Mascoto) she would decline. Most likely, Tyrone would be curious as to why she declined. Secretly she would place her hand on her stomach to let him know she was pregnant.

Kim had on a yellow sundress that tied up in the back, one her husband bought for her. He approved of it knowing that, the other women were going to be wearing similar clothing. He just asked her to put leggings under her dress, his wife looked exquisite in yellow the color complemented her hazel eyes and her butterscotch skin complexion.

Tyrone made sure he was matching his wife with his yellow polo shirt and his polo shorts. He wanted everybody to know that Kim was with him.

They left and when they got to the park, everyone else was already there. Kim pretty much knew all the wives from some of the office parties Tyrone's firm used to have. She told Tyrone she was going over to chat with them and asked if she could get him anything.

"No, Baby Girl, he replied and kissed her. He admired the glow of his wife and the flow of her body as she walked away. And he wasn't the only one.

While walking towards the wives she overheard one of his friends tell Tyrone, "Boy are you lucky you got to her first, because if I would have gotten to her that day you bought me to church she would be mine. That's a fine woman you got there. "

Unbeknownst to how Tyrone became furious over his comment, he kept going on about how Kim was gorgeous she was in her dress and how she was glowing. Kim felt her husband should have been flattered so of course, she didn't think anything of it. Because it has been times Tyrone has made a similar statement about their wives to them.

Tyrone played it cool and went along with it. But he knew when they got home; she had something coming to her. He felt his friends wouldn't have made those comments if she wasn't wearing that dress. He opts to go get some cognac to go with the Champaign he was already drinking and he drank the whole time.

Around 6 pm they got home and Kim was all ready to tell him about the baby but before she could say anything, Tyrone punched her in the mouth, and bellowed out,

"Charm is deceitful, and beauty is vain, but a woman who fears the Lord is to be praised." Proverbs 13:30

She hollered out in pain as she grabbed her mouth, "What did I do?" she asked in disbelieve

"Act as if you're available again to my friends and I'll make you the ugliest woman they have ever seen. You got that?" He snatched the yellow dress off that he brought her and it was the same dress that earlier he thought she looked so elegant and gorgeous in. She nodded her head and stood in only her panties and leggings. She had no idea what she had done but she wasn't going to do it again.

As the months passed it seemed as if Tyrone was working from home more. Kim did not question him, she feared that she would set him off. He stopped going to church and his drinking got heavier. It seemed as if an evil spirit had taken over him. By him drinking more, he became another human being. He might have stopped going to church but he quoted scriptures and twisted them to justify what he was doing or why he was hitting his wife at the time. He now called his office the room of spirits.

It had gotten to the point where she no longer was allowed to wash or go to the bathroom by herself. He wanted to be the one to touch her body and wash his vagina as he called it. His thing was once they were married the bible says she is his, Period.

Tyrone started staying out late and when he came home he found reasons to chastise Kim, to belittle her with scriptures on why she wasn't behaving like God said a wife should behave. Often he smelled her fingers and her vagina to see if she was cheating or if she touched herself in any type of way.

If she even tried to say a word to him he would hit her, punch her, or find some way to physically harm her. Each day apologizing ceased and promising to never hurt her again didn't come, anymore. He was now just giving her more scriptures of her being obedient to him and submissive.

Once they got married they went to church but she stopped studying the Bible for herself, she no longer went to the Women's church group. She relied on her husband to

provide her with the guidance and knowledge of the ways of
the bible. This much she knew was that he was the head of
household but how much was she supposed to take from
the head of household?

Kim was desperate to talk to someone Tyrone had
stopped her from getting close to the women at church. She
didn't have any friends from her past and he probably
wouldn't condone that. So, she went to Ms. Evans, if anyone
could get him to stop hitting her it should be his mother.

Kim called Ms. Evans and poured the evil doings of
her son out. She listened to Kim tell her what had been
going on. The fact that he wouldn't let her even wash herself
was something new, but she didn't dare tell Kim that. His
mother couldn't change him if she tried she wasn't able to
do it the last time. Ms. Evans was willing to do it for Kim,
she had hoped her son changed but it was evident by these
events he hasn't. Reluctantly, she told her she would talk to
him and she hops in her car to drive the two hours to Nap.

"I can't take his drinking. It's getting out of control
and I do not know what to do about it. I'm afraid to even to

look at him. I know I have to do something before he goes too far and I have a feeling he will one day. I have to leave him but I have nowhere else to go. He is all I have in this world." Ms. Evans had no idea how to help this child but she told her to do the thing that always worked: pray.

She hugged her daughter in law to comfort her and then she said to her " You need to get away from him. You can't stay in this marriage and continue to be hurt like this. He will never stop abusing you and as long as he continues to drink, it's only going to get worse. Get out while you can Kim. You can come live with me."

Kim said to her "He only acts this way because I make him mad and I say things that tick him off. I just have to learn to stay out of his way. He is busy looking for a job and he's not having any luck and I just make it unbearable for him."

Ms. Evans walked away from Kim and with her back towards her because of the shame she felt, "You don't understand, this is not Tyrone's first time doing this." She confessed

Kim was confused, "What do you mean it's not his first time?"

His mother let out a huge sigh she hoped her son had changed when she didn't get any negative phone calls from her daughter-in-law after the first year. She had thought her son had changed and turned over a new leaf. Plus they were going to church regularly, she didn't know that Tyrone was using the words of the Bible to justify the actions of man. "Tyrone was married before to a woman with a similar background as yours. Her name was Juanita. She was only 19 at the time of their marriage. Well, they only dated 6 months before they got married. As time went on, I guess he started having an affair he started drinking."

Kim had to stop and ask "what was so stressful about his job and his marriage that he would start drinking?"

"The woman he was sleeping with was a client at his firm and she was threatening to take their relationship public if he didn't leave his wife. But Juanita already had a clue about what he was doing. She got bold and started to question him about it and that's when the abuse started."

His mother confessed.

But-" Kim interrupted "Why didn't she go to the police or leave him?"

"She tried to leave him and that's when he killed her. You see my son is a very powerful man and he has a lot of people who will quickly protect him. So she was alone in what was happening. I didn't know about it until after her death when his mistress came forward and told me about his drinking problem. It appears when his wife died, she became his punching bag."

"Did you know the woman?"

"Tyrone had started bringing her around shortly after Juanita's death so I met her a few times before she came to me about Tyrone. However, I was told she was paid off. After that, I never heard from her again. And since then Tyrone hasn't been in any relationship."

Kim was in disbelief after hearing that story and all she could say was "Maybe if I didn't push him to drink he would change. I just have nobody else to turn to and I can't go back to nothing."

Understanding what her daughter in the law meant she said "Worry about your life first, leave. You have been his wife for over six years. You are entitled to everything he owes you."

Kim shook her head and said "No I can't leave him like this. Maybe this is God's way of getting him the help he needs to recover. I just have to stop bugging him about everything when he has so many things to stress over already."

Ms. Evans told her "Never blame yourself for what he is doing. All you do is love him and be there for him. You are just being a good wife. But, no woman deserves to be unhappy in their marriage. Especially not a mighty woman of God" Before his mother could finish what she was saying, Tyrone walked in the house with a case of beers and two bottles of champagne, "Mom what are you doing here?" he questioned

She just looked at Kim, who was preparing dinner and not looking at Tyrone and said "Oh nothing just came to check on my son and daughter in law. But, now that I have spent time with Kim, I need to talk to you about something."

Tyrone knew something was up, his mom avoided eye contact with him. He could see the shame and hurt on her face, he looked back and forth from his mother and his wife. His wife's back was to them so he couldn't read her. Did the partners call his mom to let her know he went too far this, time? He wondered as he followed her to his office. He imagined that his mother knew all his dark secrets, his exploitation of the Bible, using and transforming it to control his wife.

Tyrone walked over to his bar and poured him a shot of bourbon, "Mother, you look like you need a shot." He told her raising the bottle up for the offering.

Ms. Evans walks over and snatches the glass out of her son's hand, "Seems like you have been having enough of this for the both of us. Son, she continued, sincerely as she set the glass down, I thought that you learned your lesson the first time."

Tyrone let his mother win with the cup of bourbon but the bottle was coming with him, he smiled, "What do you mean mother?"

"Why are you putting your hands on your wife?" she questioned him. His mother didn't see the look of astonishment on his face, he wasn't expecting that to come out her mouth. Tyrone was furious as he listened to his mother preach he kept gulping down his liquid spirits.

"I refuse to stand by while you kill another human being. Tyrone this mess has to stop, you have to get help. You are acting just like your father." She accused.

Tyrone stood with a bottle in hand and threw the bottle inches away from his mother's head, "I am nothing like that coward. He was weak."

"I didn't raise you like this. I thought seeing what your father took me through, you would never put your hands on a woman. "

"You thought I wouldn't do that?" he laughed and took a gulp from the bottle. You stayed in the marriage, you never left him even when he put you in the hospital. So, HOW IN THE HELL DID YOU THINK I WOULDN'T BEAT MY WIFE TO SUBMISSION?"

Smack, "DON'T YOU EVER RAISE YOUR VOICE AT ME, TYRONE MATTHEW EVANS!"

"Oh, so you mad at me but you and dad taught me it was okay to put my hands on a woman, on my wife. You taught me that by staying and he taught me by doing it. And you want to smack me for putting some bass behind the truth. But not once did I ever see you hit him for hitting you. Can you explain the logic in that?" he laughed, "Can you, mother?"

"You know what; I'm going to leave before I do something to you that Juanita should have done. Trust me, son, you reap what you sow!" She snatched her purse off the counter and stormed out of the room in search of Kim.

Finding her setting the table for three, "Kim, I'm not

staying, but thank you, she said as she hugged her she whispered, I'm going to help you. Stay strong."

A shiver ran down Kim's back as the hug tightened as if that was the last time they would see each other. Kim grabbed her mother-in-law back into her embrace and whispered, "I don't know what to do and I don't know how he would react to me being ."

Tyrone's mother jerked from their embrace and grabbed her hands. The look in her eyes resembled fear, fear from Kim and fear for her unborn grandchild. Tears formed in her eyes as she placed her hand on Kim's womb, she prayed over her stomach. She removed her hand and kissed Kim on the forehead and left.

Kim removed her mother-in-law's plate and placed it back in the cabinet. She turned around and met Tyrone's fist. Kim hit the floor holding her eye.

"Tell anyone else what goes on in my house and I will

kill you. You got that?" and grabbed a bottle of wine and walked out. Kim cried on the floor and then she knew what she had to do.

That night she thought of a way to get away from him as they lay in bed. She packed her bags and set them on the porch behind some of the plants. She packed enough where he wouldn't notice she had taken much. Tomorrow night she planned on breaking away from the abusive man she married.

Kim went to sleep and she knew her life was going to change. But before she left she had to do one thing. The next day she went to the church and asked to speak with their pastor. She told him what was going on and she was at her wit's end with it all.

The pastor told her that the devil was in her marriage and that he was going to stay as long as she allowed him to. He quoted "Proverbs 10:11 The mouth of a righteous man is a well of life: but violence covereth the mouth of the wicked." He asked her how and when did this abuse start. Kim said he only started after something happened at his firm. The pastor advised her to pray for him and herself and they were in his prayers also.

Kim thanked the pastor and left. She left feeling empty and more confused. Did her pastor just tell her to stay with her abusive husband and just pray? Was she going against God by leaving her husband? Where in the bible does it say you can leave your husband if he's abusive? Divorce, bad? Is this what they mean by for Better or Worse, in Sickness and Health until Death do us part? So, when he kills me I can leave? What the hell?

Kim ventured off to Tyrone's firm, "Hello, is Mr. Briggs in?" she asked the secretary.

"Mrs. Evan's, correct?" with a slight attitude

"Attorney Donovan Briggs, Please?" Kim dismissed her question as if she was a non-factor. It was something about her attitude towards her, that she was mad at her for the one thing they had in common, her husband. That would be the only reason, they had never crossed paths before.

"Daddy, Mrs. Evansss is here," she voiced through the phone.

Mahogany wooden grand double doors opened, and a slightly older distinguish gentlemen came out with a genuine smile plastered on his face.

"Kimberley, how wonderful to see you!"

"Donovan, she greeted with a smile and a weak quivering handshake.

He frowned at the fear he had seen in her eyes, "Step into my office Kim, ushering her into his office, Miss Briggs hold my calls and can you please stop calling me Daddy. Let's keep it professional." He scolded his daughter.


Kim stepped into their home greeted with Tyrone waiting on the couch with yet another drink in his hand. That was all he seemed to be consuming for the last month. Now, talking to Donovan she knew why. Kim placed the call to Ms. Evans.

"Hey, Baby! I went out and got us takeout from your

favorite restaurant.

Tyrone gave a drunken attempt to stand and when Kim came into the living room, "Where in hell have you been all day?"

"Well, I had a couple of errands to run. I went by to see Pastor Bryant." She said going towards the kitchen.

Tyrone grabbed her by the hair yanking her backward sending the food tumbling onto the white carpet.

"Don't you lie to me, you whore. Jezebel! No, you're Delilah! You were out with another man. I can see it in your face. Did you make plans with Donovan too? Oh, you thought I wouldn't find out? You can't take a shit and wipe your ass without me knowing." He laughed hysterically while pulling her hair harder and started to punch her repeatedly.

"Stoppppp it, she cried

He shoved her to the ground and when she hit the floor she heard her arm pop. She cried out in pain and it was at that moment she saw death in her husband's eyes.

He was going to kill her if she didn't defend herself. Kim tried to move away from him and get to the kitchen, but he was too fast for her.

While she tried to get away he told her "By the way, if you think you can leave me, you got another thing coming. I found your bags on the porch and why did my mother call here saying to meet her at 8:30 tonight huh? You, think I was going to let you go that easy? Oh no, you are going to be with me until death do us part. And if that day has come tonight then consider us parted. Because I refuse to be Hosea! Yeah, the Holy Spirit tried to warn me about you. And the Lord himself came to me and said Kill her if she tries to leave."

"Oh, you mean the way you did Juanita and all your women? Huh, you want to kill me like you did her? What's going on with you and Donovan's daughter?" She kept throwing questions at him to buy her some time as he chased her around the living room. She was tripping over his liquor bottles.

Tyrone started grabbing liquor bottles off the floor

throwing them at Kim. Swoosh, she ducked as the bottles came swooshing by her head shattering into the wall behind her. She screamed out in pain and kept dodging and inching her way towards the kitchen. All the while, he kept trying to hit her with bottles. When she finally made it to the kitchen, she tried to block her fear out and keep herself focused on the knives. She moved over to the counter and quickly grabbed the knife. Tyrone made it to the kitchen still stumbling but ready to begin his drunken violent torrent towards his wife. When her husband saw what she was doing, he punched her in the stomach and when she fell to the floor, the knife flew out of her hand.

She kicked him in the leg to get a chance to get back to the knife. He recovered quickly and came after her grabbing her by the feet and pulling her closer to him. He choked her until her face turned blue and once she was gasping for air, he picked her up by her throat and tried to fling her across the room with all the strength he could muster. She hit the countertops ribs and stomach first before her body crashed on the marble floor.

Kim felt something wet run and surge down her legs, a pain lanced through her from her stomach to her legs. Looking down, it hit her that she was losing their baby. In his bare feet, Tyrone felt the sticky blood beneath his feet as he rushed towards her. He did not care. He didn't even look down to see the crimson colored liquid spilling from his wife's womb. He swung but Kim's adrenaline kicked in, she mustered up the strength to hit him in his stomach before he could hit her again.

It worked because he grabbed his stomach and she tried to regain her composure. When she did, she grabbed the knife and stabbed him in the arm. He fell against the counter crying out in pain. She charged him and continued to try to stab him as he blocked her swings with the knife. One of his hits connected with the side of her head. She cried out as she hit the back of her head on the floor.

For a brief minute, she envisioned that she was still stabbing him. He fell to the ground and he lay on his back in pain. She stood over him and he said "You don't have it in your heart to hurt the only man who ever really loved you" He gloated.

She thought to herself "this isn't the way love is supposed to be."

She remembered her mother and how she vowed to never be like her. She kept thinking "All I did was love him and he let alcohol turn him into a monster and hurt the woman he claimed to be his wife. But I won't allow him to hurt me anymore. He'll never be able to hurt me again." And with that thought, she shoved the knife into his heart. She watched her husband take his last breath and when he did, she got a bottle of champagne and placed it next to him and said: "drink up." The yelling ceased and the hitting as he looked down to see what was warm and sticky on his bare feet.

Kim woke up from her brief blackout and came back to her reality. Her husband was staring at her with a bewildered look on his face. She felt the wetness of what he was looking at and looked between her legs. Her heart ached.

He looked at her without any words, he knew he was drunk out of his mind but he couldn't be beating her that bad. Not enough to have all this blood on soaking up his floor.

Kim was on the floor crying and screaming, "I'M LOSING OUR BABY, OH MY GOD MY BABY!" In shock, no longer caring about the beating she just endured or if he was coming at her with more. She coiled up in a fetal position, sobbing in pain from losing her child. "YOU KILLED OUR CHILD YOU MONSTER!" She yelled at Tyrone as she finally started to pull herself along the floor to get to the phone by the chair. Nobody had ever been pregnant; he would have never hit her if she would have told him. Not his first wife, none of his girlfriends or mistresses.

Tyrone realizing what was going on, his sobriety hit him fast and the pain hit him even harder as he fell to his knees in a puddle of his unborn child. He grabbed the knife that was lost in the shuffle and a bottle of Jack Daniels off of the table, with his child's blood on his hands and feet, he zoned out as he staggered towards the chair his wife was trying to reach, he left bloody footprints next to his wife's smears of blood on the floor. He gulped down the liquid, "No, no, he whispered, he had no scriptures to justify killing his unborn child; he continued to drink and talk to himself as he slowly dragged his stumbling feet towards the chair.

The violent emotional roller coaster that both were going through was enough to bring seventy demons into the room, bringing war to their spirits. This time and maybe this time those demons was going to overcome the spirit that those misused scriptures fractured in Kim.

Her thoughts were not of a woman of God, they were evil, her thoughts envisioned killing him to background music, her mind wanted to kill him slowly, and then pray over every wound she gave to his body. She wanted to destroy him slowly like he has done to her spirit over these last months. She watched him as he ignored her laying there bleeding, she feared what he would do to her next but her hatred at this point was incredible with a mighty strength, that she didn't know was in her. She steady pulled her body along the floor, no longer caring what Tyrone was doing. In her mind, she needed to get to the phone to save her child before it was too late.

Tyrone wanted nothing but for this pain to go away, he had never felt this pain. Once he reached the chair, he plopped down and let the liquor spill on him. He looked at his wife, looked at the phone and then gulped down his spirits in the bottle. For some reason, this bottle must have been more potent than anything he had before or maybe it was the realization of what he had done that had him in another zone. He continued to move his eyes from his wife to the knife, to the phone.

He no longer wanted to live, how could he had let his gluttony of drinking spirits and the spirit of misusing the bible scriptures to his advantage. Didn't God say he was head of household he was only trying to bring her to submission, mold her to be the wife he wanted her to be? He knew he fell into his old ways like with Juanita, but if she would have just told him she was pregnant then he would have ceased all actions. Well at least all physical abuse, would have stopped until she had their child.

There was no verse in the Bible to handle this, to get him out of this, to save his soul or mind from this. His soul cried out a painful haunting call to God as he spread the blood on his tear stricken face. By this time Kim had reached the phone, she careful stretched her hand out for it. Tyrone grabbed her hand a pulled her up to him, terrified Kim looked wild-eyed at him. He placed the blade in her hand and leaned down for her to reach his throat. He placed the tip of the blade to his Adam's apple, pleading with his eyes for her to slide it across his throat.

Kim had flashes of what he put her through over the past months, she gripped the knife the demons entertained her with thoughts of payback, but she remembered Romans 12:19 and she wasn't going to hell for her husband.

Kim saw tears in Tyrone's eyes as he took another swig of the alcohol to drain it of all its evil spirits. He let alcohol turn him into a monster again. He thought of all the scriptures he had twisted to fit and uplift his manhood and his position as the head of household intertwined with the lust and the alcohol, he had ruined his life with the Gluttony of Spirits.

Tyrone couldn't stand to be on this earth knowing he had killed his unborn child, so to him, he had to take the coward's way out. He wanted to burn in hell for all eternity; he grabbed the knife back from his wife. He said a prayer for her and their child and asked God for forgiveness. Tyrone plunged the knife into his abdomen and dragged it across to the other side; Kim watched on in astonishment as she saw her husband spit out blood and his insides spill onto the floor next to the fetus of their child.


Proverbs 23:2  And put a knife to your throat if you are given an appetite

TakeOver Publishing

# The King and the Pawn

## By

## Green eyed Puerta Rican

## Chapter 1

Cameron was sitting in the passenger seat of Mainy's aunt's old school ride when Mainy's OG challenged him on some paper that he felt wasn't owed to him. They argued back and forth about what cut was who's until it escalated to the big OG calling Mainy's mom a hoe.

"I heard that shit like I was standing right there," Cam said as he looked at his friend. "I mean, right as I looked up from my phone is when he had hit cuz so hard that he knocked him outstanding straight the fuck up. I swear for God my nigga, he was dead ass asleep. Shit was weird cuz."

Tory laughed at the story and said, "You bullshitten nigga. That shit ain't possible"

"It was like his brain hadn't told his muscles shit yet. It was so fucking crazy mah dude." Cam laughed, so hard every time he was retelling the story. That story had basically turned him into an urban legend of sorts.

"So he was literally still standing up?" Tory asked as if he had to still believe the words for himself.

"On everything my nigga," he said as he took a bite into some garlic mashed potatoes. Cam lived for food. No one on this earth loved food as he did. Mainy guessed it was all those years in the struggle. He was always eating something, and if it weren't for his job and his age he would be fat as fuck.

"Shit!  How long did cuz stay like that?"

"Until Mainy pushed him over"

"Cuz." he dragged out the C.

"For reals. Everyone stood there in shock until cuz's body hit the concrete like a giant sack of potatoes"

No one had ever seen no shit like that before. Especially coming from a youngsta like him. The kid was only seventeen-years-old.

"Damn, that's some crazy shit."

People thought at first it was a fluke. They'd thought that their Big OG had just got caught by surprise or some shit.

"He had a glass jaw," Tre said.

Their Big OG had been knocking mutha fukkas out forever. He was nigga everyone looked up to. That is until the one day, that one nanosecond when Mainy robbed their Big OG from all the clout he had built up for years.

Mainy began his climb to the top of the food chain. Once he started mopping fools up left and right, homies were losing respect for the leaders of their corners, their turf captains and their OGs. Niggas started stashing their dope and guns when they saw that Mainy was coming around and most of them motherfuckers didn't want any parts of Mainy.

Truth be told he was untrustworthy. He was like that one lion in the pride who would not bow to any other. He didn't care about anything. There wasn't anything in this world that he felt he would die for, and a small few he would kill for. He was cold-blooded.

"Who the fuck wanted to get punked by a seventeen-year-old? No one, that's the fuck who. That shit would hurt your pride like a motherfucker," Tre said right before he slammed back a glass of cognac.

Cameron and Mainy's big homie Tre laughed together. Tre had heard some parts of the story before, but he thought it was just some fairytale that motherfuckers had been telling for years.

Cameron was Mainy's oldest and truest friend. He remembered hearing about Mainy's biggest takeovers, and that day he told Cam that he wanted him to be a part of Mainy's Empire, it was at Pappadeaux's while eating some

Branzino on a half shell. He'd never eaten anything like that before, and that first bite opened Cam's eyes to the realest possibilities in his life. He'd never be able to afford this life, not on his salary. Sometimes he had envied Mainy. He had wished he could trade his old promises for a new reality. Mainy's tales from the hood was unbelievable if Cam hadn't been there for most of it he wouldn't believe it either. Mainy and his hustling abilities amazed Cameron. The money was flowing like champagne at a Billionaires Club.

Cam was never a gang banger. He wasn't even a hustler. He was a loyal friend who was there for Mainy when Mainy had experienced some of the most fucked up shit a kid could ever deal with. Like him, Cam was given a raw deal in life. Mainy was short fused, bitter, and sometimes way out of control, he needed a brother with a good head on his shoulders. Someone who could blend, someone who didn't blow his top, after all, Cameron grew up playing it safe. He was a good guy and Mainy trusted him with his secrets and his life, and that was saying a lot because Mainy didn't trust anyone.

Cameron was a square but there wasn't a question of whether or not he was enticed by the money. He loved how it made him feel. The power he felt behind those Benjamin's. The bitches, the way in which women jocked him when he rode in Mainy's whips, when he entered the clubs, making it rain. He loved it, he thrived in it.

The Executive Suites were at his disposal, he could go to most five-star restaurants and not wait. How many black men could say that? These white folks had no idea that all of it was earned from the sweat of one nigga's brow. The dirt that had paved the way for half the shit he had. Cameron felt like a star and if he had to cross some lines to handle shit, he would. As a matter of fact. after many, many years....he did.

## Chapter 2

Cameron had love for his Mama more than anybody on this earth and in the same breath, he hated his father just that much more. His mother told him at an early age that his father was dead, and that he wasn't worth knowing anyway, so his mother was the only family he ever really knew. He'd heard the rumors in the streets about the Legend, the man that pro-created him. Some men spoke highly of him, but most said his father was as heartless as the devil himself.

It wasn't until he turned twelve when his mother revealed to him the true-life facts about his father and all the bullshit he'd done while she was carrying him in her young womb. That's when his obsession initiated. The flame that would engulf his anger into blue hot rage. He became engrossed in the thought of one-day getting revenge. See, apparently, his father was said to be his father but wasn't truly his father. She explained to him how she was young and stupid and the first time she'd laid eyes on BT she knew it would end up being the worst decision she'd ever make.

BT was loud and boisterous, he let it be known that he was nothing but a straight savage and that he was not to be trusted, period.

Men feared him and women were turned on by him, right before they were turned out. The reality made Cameron sick to his stomach.

Cameron took a different path in life, he was forced into a life that he felt would never be his caliber. He'd been poor for most of his upbringing and it made him sick. He had a clear hatred for everyone else that had obtained all the material things he'd wished to acquire. Niggas killed other niggas over sneakers and dope sacks, he actually understood it. Survival of the fittest but he couldn't just be a street nigga. He took an oath, an oath that would later cause him an internal Civil war.

It was 1994 Vanessa was an only child of a mother who didn't know how to show her how to be a respectful young woman. Hell, her mother was a young mother herself, and Vanessa spent more time alone then she'd ever spent with anyone else.  The neighbors who lived on the first floor of her apartment building were always live. They were that crib that had all the company and all the drama. Vanessa's Mom thought it was a dope spot at first and usually made sure to switch her ass on by most the ballers when she saw them out there on the lawn.


This day, Vanessa just happened to be watching them downstairs in the Courtyard shooting dice. BT or as most called him Big Turf had long silky hair to his shoulders and big, pretty almond shaped eyes. She'd never been with a man before but that didn't mean she didn't know when one was fine.

It was hot outside and the moment BT shed his t-shirt Vanessa felt something she had never felt before, she peered through the blinds at his naked frame, his sublime

Chocolate skin. She was entranced by the way people

reacted to him and the more she studied him the faster the

heartbeat between her legs pulsated.

That day she thought BT and her eyes had caught

each other somewhere in between her peering through the

blind and him looking in his general vicinity. That was how

young girls thought. BT was in his late twenties at the time

and thought he was God's gift to pussy.

Vanessa was sure that BT was nothing like anyone

she'd ever met before and watched him from afar. BT also

kept his eye on her but never took stock of anything ever

coming about it. He thought she appeared to be smart and

mature for her young age.

One day while Vanessa was picking up some soda and chips at the little corner store. Some teen boy from her school bumped into her spilling her bags over and onto the floor and had the fucking nerve to tell her to watch out. BT noticed, it was an immature play the boy thought would get some play but he was dead wrong. Big Turf just happens to pop his way into the store for a pack of squares when he saw little Vanessa on the ground trying to gather up her bags.

Vanessa had tears coming down her face she was partly embarrassed and partly pissed. She hated those immature ass boys. She thought about how they'd all be sorry for treating her that way, she had big plans for her future.

Vanessa remembered the power she once saw in a courtroom against her mother's cousin. She dreamt of the thought of being able to have that power over everyone who's ever done her wrong or looked past her because of her Mom or their situation. After all, she was young and her mind hadn't fully developed.

BT bent down and helped gather up her stuff. He generally was uncaring but something about Vanessa made him test his boundaries he almost didn't care that the thoughts he was having, were different to him, almost nurturing, she smiled up at him and every time her eyes met his, she, in turn, imagined what he looked like without his shirt. She thought about his physique and how it made her feel. How she wanted to touch places on him that she'd never even seen before, places that she could only imagine.

BT ignored the obvious fascination she showed to him and sent her on her merry little way, he even offered to give her more money if she needed it, as long as she stayed out of the streets.

## Chapter 3

### Four years later

BT wasn't who he was before, now he didn't have to do any corner hustling or get his hands dirty in the streets. He was the shot caller now in the pussy game. He had a little stable of females that would sell their souls for him, a little weed, a meal, and some good dick was all some of the hood girls needed back then. Now, the money he accumulated off of selling dope back then, gave him the luxury to acquire expensive things to lure the crème' de le crème of women into his stable. It also helped him turn those hood girls into the cream of the crop also.

Vanessa was fresh out of high school with a scholarship to a choice college. Her hard work and staying away from the streets was taking her places, she knew exactly what she wanted in life. Big Turf watched Vanessa closely and he knew how summertime before College could break a young girl if they weren't strong-minded enough. BT wanted her to stay the course for his own selfish reasons. He hoped she would go into Law like she had once mentioned to him.

BT pulled up on Vanessa outside the Projects. Everyone knew BT's car because of his personalized plates that read Tru2turf and called her over to his ride. Where he congratulated her and gave her an envelope containing two G's.

"I heard about your accomplishments. Thought I should give you something, I mean I'm proud of you baby girl. I watched you make it even though you had a rough ride." He said with a smile.

His smile was sexier than she ever imagined and even as a legal adult with a few life experiences under her belt, he still stirred something inside of her. Just his presence could bring a fiery puddle of juices in her panties that she wished he would come and extinguish. She was legit fascinated by him and the thought of his dick.

He'd been watching her stage performance all the way from the balcony so to speak. He knew she'd be a Grammy award-winning actress when he was done with her.

"I can't take this money," She said, peeking inside the envelope once more, but the excitement of the money made her smile light up like a five-carat diamond.

"Yes you can, hard work pays, and you've earned it baby girl." Vanessa felt her heart jump in her chest. She stared into his handsome face, lost in the smooth velvety chocolate complexion; she still wished she could have more time with him. So she could show him what kind of a woman she'd grown into. Not just mentally, but the fact that her curves made most men salivate showed her that she could control any situation if she wanted too, and at the moment he was the situation she wanted to be in. He seemed preoccupied, by the women in the neighborhood and his phone was blowing up as if he was the Potus. "what the fuck?" she thought to herself.

She hoped that one day he would see her for more than that little girl from around the way, after all, she was officially a woman. BT looked her over and said, He whispered something in her ear. They stood in a haze of sexual air, then he spouted off, "Do the right thing" before he looked over both his shoulders, checking his surroundings, and hopped into his BENZ screeching off. Leaving a young Vanessa standing there with more money than ever and also insatiable desire to want to fuck the shit out of BT.

If only she knew where that money came from and what his true intentions for her actually were. She would have kept her mind focused and her legs closed. Vanessa

was a virgin, but only she knew that.  So, she thought. But

naïve to how the hood works, she thought her secret was

known to only her. In the hood virgin or hoe, the word

spread like warm butter on bread.

The next day at a private party for many of the elite

graduates from her school, some people she recognized and

some she didn't. Dorian stood on a balcony by himself

overlooking the city nightscape. The moon was gigantic in

the night sky and after she first shared words with Dorian,

because actually, she thought he was cute. He had nice

waves, smooth skin, and gorgeous teeth. She had a thing

for nice teeth. He was well liked and smooth, a ladies man

who up until that moment never really noticed how sexy

Vanessa had become.

This was the first time he'd seen her with her hair

down and a little bit of makeup. Vanessa stayed in the

books and wasn't impressed by any guy at her school. Boys were aware of Vanessa's beauty but at that age they wanted everything to come easy, they didn't want to work for the pussy. And Vanessa would have been too much work. Dorian and Vanessa picked up a conversation, Vanessa was smiling more than usual and laughing. Money had that effect. Dorian seemed cool too. They talked about rap, The 90's East coast West coast beef. Both of them were big PAC fans.

The drinks were flowing and the joints were in heavy rotation. Next thing they knew it was four am in the morning. That's when Vanessa's dress was above her waist and Dorian's mouth was doing incredible things to her vagina. The entire time she had envisioned that it was actually BT. The way his mouth looked the night before when he gave her the money. Dorian's mouth on her pussy was as far as she wanted to go. But, she was dumb and drunk and didn't stop Dorian as he entered inside of her raw.

Although Vanessa imagined BT inside of her, Dorian's sex game couldn't be anything like the veteran BT's and it left Vanessa in a pool of vomit and regrets the next day. She felt a little embarrassed. How could she just give it up like that after all those years? Did she know why? She never let anything happen without having a small part in it and that night she let alcohol and the longing for BT, let Dorian and his up and coming NBA Career get between her legs and get the best of her.

She never got a text back. And that's why she never wanted to fuck with someone as young minded as Dorian. she knew the moment she gave him her pussy there wouldn't be anything left between them.

Six-weeks later while in the Japanese Hibachi spot Vanessa spotted Dorian. "Hey, Vanessa spoke nervously."

"What's up, Vanessa?" Dorian said while giving her a hug.

"Well, she said, looking timidly around the crowded restaurant hoping no one could hear her. "I'm pregnant." Vanessa didn't know how the star player was going to act towards her confession. He had a big future in front of him and she knew it had been rumors of other girls trying to trap him by falsifying their pregnancies. She, on the other hand, was telling the truth, after all, she also had a bright future in front of her. Her becoming pregnant the summer before she went off to College was not a decision she would have made. She had a full ride because of her 4.0 academic career.

Dorian clenched his teeth as he gave Vanessa a reassuring hug, "How about I come over later and we can talk about it one on one?"

Vanessa relaxed and smiled, "Sure." But something in his facial expression made her wish she never had to confess those words.

*Later that day*

Vanessa made sure her mother was not at home, she greeted Dorian with a smile on her face. Dorian lunged at her and picked her up by her throat, through clenched teeth, he voiced his true feelings, "I'm tired of all y'all bitches coming at me because I'm going to the NBA. So, I'm going to tell you like all those other lying hoes. Ain't no dumb little hood bitch gonna ruin my future. You threw me the pussy I caught it, and before that, you slipped away with that older nigga. I don't know what the fuck happened with that So, what happens after that is your mother fucking problem. But, just in case," he took his right hand from around her neck and punched her in the stomach.

Vanessa took in every word he said to her while gasping for air and clawing at his hands around her throat. The hit to her stomach brought tears to her eyes, the pain had to have damaged her growing fetus. Dorian spitefully spit down on her scrunched up body, if that hit didn't work he was hoping the venom from his spit finished the job and he walked out of her apartment. Five minutes had passed since Dorian left her apartment before she could muster up the strength to stand.  Trying to catch her breath she sobbed violently, clutching her stomach. Carefully she walked into the bathroom, checked herself to make sure there wasn't any show of blood between her legs.

She looked at herself in the mirror, she hated the defeated look in her eyes. She was on her own and her future plans were dead. "Fucking pussy." She spat! She had to make new plans and she knew exactly what to do.

The next night a black limousine rolled up to her crib. Vanessa got in and took off. The nosey bitch upstairs immediately picked up her landline and made a call.

## Chapter 4

Vanessa wasn't as dumb and naive as most people would think.

She was an only child with a neglectful Mom and absentee Dad; she had no choice but to become her own hero. Vanessa observed her surroundings, playing dumb when they approached her with that street shit. Only displaying her book smarts around people. She was going to be a survivor by any means. So she made sure her attire spoke volumes, with the sexy Mandarin Collar Lace-up Hollowed-out Gold Two-piece Skirt Set, with the lace-up gold stilettos, it was her mother's outfit but Vanessa filled it out even better. her Mother was one badass bitch, she was one to be reckoned with but Vanessa turned into something quite unexpected and once scorned the entire game plan would become one of the Queens. She wasn't dumb and that played favor to all her soon-to-be hustles.

The limousine pulled up to a downtown building. The building was huge and almost smelled of old money it was one of those buildings like the one you see in the movies with a doorman and the whole nine yards. It kind of turned Vanessa on, empowered her to do what she had to do. Everything she had inside of her had suddenly switched to a different mindset.

She was on that fuck a mother fucker mindset. It was a dog eat dog world and she will never forget how she was led to water but her teacher never taught her to drink. She was on her own like she' been most of her young life.

The doorman opened the back door to the limo he looked at her smooth sexy thighs as she stepped out to the curb, then he watched her as she maneuvered her stilettos on the marble floor leading to his Penthouse Suite. He was use to turning the hood girls and the bookworms into butterflies, but Vanessa already had transformed herself into the ideal woman for any man. She handled herself with such class, unlike all the other women he usually kept company with.

BT had wanted this day for a very long time and when it was time, he'd sent for her without hesitation.

Vanessa swallowed hard before she knocked on the door, she'd also been anticipating this day forever. It had been some time since she'd laid eyes on him. She'd been doing her thang, she'd become a woman with experiences and big ideas. She was nothing like the girl he had once bribed with an envelope of dead presidents.

BT's bodyguard opened the door for Vanessa, he bit his lip as he eyed her from the tip of her toes to the tip of her nose. She was bad as fuck, he thought to himself. She wished he would try. But he knew better than to even attempt to approach her, Big Turf will have his head.

BT told Jay, he could bounce for the night. Big Turf had anticipated a great night full of surprises. He watched his beautiful sexy companion sashay into the Executive Suite. It was a hot summer night and the material of her five hundred dollar outfit was sticking to her gorgeous body. Her nipples were poking through the peekaboo lace in her dress. BT's dick was hard enough to cut through wood itself. He wanted her pretty little ass. He locked the door behind him and went to the bar for a couple of glasses of Irish whiskey and some coke.

After a few drinks, the alcohol loosened a tear or two.

"Baby Girl, What's going on? I thought we were having a good time."

Vanessa looked up and weakly smiled, "I am, BT! I'm just disappointed in myself." She confessed her secret about getting pregnant and how Dorian reacted to his problem with her pregnancy. How she spent months inside a dope spot, slanging dubs and taking online exams, while her young seed grew inside her stomach. How'd she'd felt so alone, no father, no mother, no deadbeat ass baby daddy. BT wheels started turning, he had remembered when she wasn't that far along but he thought sending in another young girl to try to talk sense into Dorian could still get him a nice payday from the young baller if they played their cards right. In his dreams, BT saw dollar signs tattooed on Vanessa's growing belly. He'd blackmail his ass to the press about his wrongdoings, his domestic violence. But Vanessa disappeared he had word on the street that she was slanging, yay and pills. The truth was they said she had that neighborhood on lock, she paid some young hitters to watch her back.

BT had been in Vanessa's ear for a little over an hour, about how sorry he was their plan didn't work out the way it was supposed to. When they were interrupted by a buzz at the door. BT got up an answered the door letting in another young lady. Josie walked in like an Amazon and she was displaying all of her assets boldly. She was really pretty and tall; Vanessa remembered thinking as she strutted in making eye contact with BT and Vanessa.

"Vanessa, Josie. Josie, Vanessa. Down." He said eyeing Josie. As Josie unzipped BT's zipper with her teeth and unbuttoned his pants, BT locked eyes with Vanessa,

"Watch," he demanded her. Despite the shock value of Josie being uninhibited enough to suck a man's dick with an audience, Vanessa was turned on immensely that wasn't sweat between her legs. She had never done anything like that before. She felt some type of way as she watched the performance and BT gave commentary on how to give a man a mind-blowing blowjob.

After she finished BT gave her a small bag of cocaine and the girl went into the bathroom with it. Snorted a couple of lines and cleaned herself up. Josie walked past Vanessa and their eyes met, Josie shook her head trying to give Vanessa a warning. Josie might have looked bold and fearless but she wasn't. She was ashamed of herself for what she had become, she was in the same predicament Vanessa was in just a year prior.

Vanessa squints her eyes trying to decipher why Josie was shaking her head. BT turned around trying to figure out what Vanessa was looking at but Josie quickly turned her head forward and kept walking right out the door.

BT had been turning women out for years, his original plan for Vanessa was for her to take a personal interest and become his lawyer, but she fucked that up by losing her focus and deciding to do whatever she wanted. This enraged him; she would have been the biggest asset in his criminal empire. He wasn't going to waste all those years he spent grooming her from afar, she was going to pay him back just like the rest of these hoes. Just like her mother.

## Chapter 5

Vanessa had sex with BT and then she slipped a strong muscle relaxer in his drink. He was on the bed snoring like he was a bear in hibernation. Vanessa tiptoed over to the door and slide the chain opening the door. Vanessa's mother stood there half naked and nervous.

She was holding a three-year-old child, who Josie referred to as Mainy.

"Come on Mommy' we got this. She said taking Mainy from Jada's arms and passing her to Josie. They all were afraid and angry at that same time.

Vanessa's mom Jada reached inside of BT's shoe and underneath the sole she found a key pulled it out and walked over to a safe in the closet. Where they robbed him blind.

"For all the bullshit ass years, mother fucker"

"Piece of shit."

As they grabbed anything of value and wiped away prints.

Jada walked over to where he slept and stuck the silencer in his mouth and put his lights completely out without hesitation. She wished she had never met his punk ass.

Vanessa did everything she could to free her mom but it was never enough he wanted Jada, Vanessa, Josie he wanted the money of the young NBA player. He wanted the heart and souls of any women he could get a hold of. He wasn't shit and he deserved what he got and even more.

They raised Mainy and Cam like brothers, they were bonded for life because of their mothers. The women wanted them to be a force to be reckoned with, they wanted them to be better than the Dorian's and BT's of the world.

Unfortunately, Mainy and Cam found Josie dead with a needle in her arm when Mainy was in the second grade, It was the worst day of Mainy's life. He was never the same after that. Mainy became who he had become and Cam took a different path.

Then one day after a few lines, a zany and some drank. Cam suddenly realizes that he feels like he should have more of the money than Mainy's been giving him. After all, his mother saved Mainy and Mainy's mother and he was the one risking his life out there as a dirty ass cop. Risking life and limb for niggas that could kill him if the word Police fell from anyone's lips.

So he confronts Mainy as if Mainy wouldn't do anything for him, Cam doesn't realize that Mainy has been watching Cam's descent into the darkness.

He knows, he's been trying to double cross him, it's hurting him because he was the only real friend he thought he had, he was his brother, and two minutes before he pulls the trigger he lets Cam knows that he always shared all the money, that he had an offshore account for the both of them so one day they both could leave the streets. Cam confesses that Mainy must be jealous because he knew that Cameron had a real father, that he knew Cam always fantasized about his legendary basketball-playing father.

That he would one day walk back into his life and tell him how sorry he was and let him live the life of a millionaire's son.

But the truth was as he pulls back the hammer, "Everyone knows you were just the pimp's son. Just like me nigga. BT fathered us both, your mother should've told you the truth"

"You no good greedy ass mother fucker! Don't you know at the end of the game, The King and the Pawn both go back into the same box."

Mainy pulled the hammer back as he pointed to Cam's head."

Boom!!!!

# Evil Brain Angel Heart

# By

# E.B.A.H.

## Chapter 1

Man walks into church, lured by the deep baritone voice of a man preaching, "There are six things the Lord hates, seven that are detestable to him: haughty eyes, a lying tongue, hands that shed innocent blood, a heart that devises wicked schemes, feet that are quick to rush into evil, a false witness who pours out lies and a man who stirs up dissension among brothers" The baritone preacher was animated with every word.

Behind him stood an unmoving chorus cloaked in gold, standing their ground like soldiers ready to attack any adversaries that came through that door. The man in his bloody Timberlands, bloody hands, would not dare himself to soil a seat beyond the back. Something in him told him to stay close to the doors, just in case, God did not see his evil feet fit to cross over into his holy sanctuary and set flame to his flesh. HE was delusional into believing that he could just run out of the church, stop, drop and roll to the fire hydrant he passed by in front of the church and put out the flames of God. The preacher repeated Proverbs 6:16.-`19, louder and more animated like a southern preacher. It sent chills even through his scheming wicked heart, so why wasn't the congregation moving. Why wasn't there a, "Yes, Lawd," "Preach", "Gone Preacher", coming from their holier than thou lips? Sister so and so wasn't falling out catching the Holy Ghost. Unmoving statues of faith or flesh were sitting right in front of him, immune to the word. But just there to say they heard it. Just there to say they were there in the house of the Lord.

He was curious about their identities, he stood and the chorus raised their arms slowly with their index fingers pointed towards him. He took a step and the motionless congregation whipped their heads back towards him. He fell to his knees, his heart was beating like African drums. The scream of disbelief was caught in his throat, his bloodstained hands dripped blood as he covered his eyes from his haunting shame. The flashes of his truth insulted his mind, He remembers when he robbed the drug dealer to indulge in the drug for free. He was too lazy to hustle or get a job. His wife took care of him. Even with a family to take care of, he never had a 9 to 5. He always hustled and he hustled big in the streets. But doing a ten-year bid he was no longer at the top of the food chain.

Besides his new habit had him in a choke hold he couldn't maneuver his way out of. He remembers spreading it on the kitchen table, sniffing each line without thinking about the consequences of gluttony. His phone indicates he has a text message just as his wife walked in with a disgusted look on her face. He checked his messages and there in the video was his wife giving the drug dealer head. Rage built up inside of him, he looked at the lines and he lusted after it and snorted. That last snort sent him over the edge.

He watched the video again as he calmly walked to the closet and loaded his gun. He did not once notice her tears, the look of shame, the fact that the man he stole from was thrusting upwards while he had his hands wrapped around her head shoving her head down, the choking and vomit did not register in his mind.

He ran back in the room where his wife was to find her kneeling and praying. She was praying for him. He pressed the gun to her head and pulled the trigger. He cupped her head as to not let her body hit the ground, he laid her there softly. Lifeless was her beauty, her brains were decorating their dull walls with red brightness with pink under hues. He thought, even in death his wife could add beauty to any room that she was in. he left her dead, as he ran out of the house like a roaring beast.

Back to his subconscious guilt covered reality, their faces all of their faces were his wife's face. The whole congregation held the beauty of his dead wife, including his last touch of a bullet hole in her head. Anger seized him as he pulled out his gun again, ready to kill again. He would kill her over and over again for sharing what was his, for giving another man part of her body. It was his right as her husband to punish her as he sees fit. God can't send me to hell for that. he told himself because seeing her dead face was his hell. His phone rang again as the chorus slowly walked towards him pointing their fingers, he quickly looked at his messages and another video came up with his wife pleading with the man he had crossed, "Please don't kill my husband. I'm sorry for what he did. I will do anything, just don't kill him."

The drug dealer laughed, "Your pretty ass has to perform fellatio on me or that mother fucker is dead. And not just today, any day that I want it done, and anywhere you will fall to your knees and put me in your mouth." he told her unzipping his pants, grabbing her hair and shoving her down to her knees.

He then puts the camera in his face, "You scheming, lying thieving ass mother fucker. You steal from me, I take something of yours. Eye for an eye mother fucker. For the rest of your life, you are going to have to deal with the image of my dick in your wife's mouth and you are the reason she's swallowing my babies." The video ended.

Not once did he stop to think, it was his fault. The chorus had surrounded him as the Preacher repeated the scripture. The congregation baring her beautiful face started chanting an Eye for an Eye.

The Preacher stepped down from the pulpit with the face of his son, no longer preaching about, what God hates. He's now preaching to him in a child-like voice, "You killed my mother. You killed my mother. The church was set to flames as he turned the gun to his head and but his cowardliness would not let him pull the trigger, Boom, nevertheless it was pulled and he lay lifeless in the sanctuary of the Lord.

## Chapter 2

I refuse to dominate this killing spirit that is in me, I let it take over because I rely on it, I demand it's darkness for revenge on an enemy who had the audacity to reach inside my soul and hold it captive. You say he can't know God. He can't know the Bible because clearly, it says "Vengeance is mine sayeth the Lord." But the killing spirit in me has whispered to me that my GOD has also said, "And thine eye shall not pity; but life shall go for life, eye for an eye, tooth for tooth, hand for hand, and foot for foot."

The Old Testament has my heart and mind succumbing to its BC (Before Christ) ways. In this world of torment and treachery, I would surely perish if I lived my life following the New Testament of Jesus's repudiates of an eye for an eye and I turn the other cheek. When my work is done, I will throw myself on the altar and repent to the Lord and announce my deeds of street justice.

Until then, I will coil out the eyes of men who seek pleasure in their recreational unjust acts of bloodshed. I will smite them with my multitude of weapons that will surely create their demise in a harrowing way. I don't need your approval, I don't need your comprehension of my tactics. Just thank me when your streets are rid of miscreants, butchers of our children and their innocence degenerates who take pleasure in violating our women and the drug traffickers who profit and delivers the misguiding euphoria of slow death. I will take pride in their slaughtering as you will secretly take solace in knowing I am lurking somewhere near ready to protect the innocent.

I have no father or mother to teach me right from wrong for my mother died by my father's hands and my father by mine. I was 9 years old when I first sought street justice. You could say my first taste of the peculiar savoring taste of murder was acquired by this event. I continued to seek it.

Now at the age of 13, I hunt for the man on the video that lay playing next to my father's dead body. Until I find him I will leave a path of blood that would lead me to him like the yellow brick road that leads Dorothy to The Wiz. I am a man but not yet a man in this society's standards. My face will delude you into believing that my innocence was still intact and that alone will bring my enemy out to seek me to do his evil bidding of handing out deadly euphoria to my community. And I would place myself in front of my enemy and watch as God places a table before him as I devour my meal which is of him. My meat his flesh, my sides his soul and my wine his blood and I will stand before the rest of his minions and wipe my hands with his heart. My belly will be full, my hunger satisfied.

## Chapter 3

Sloth watched the young boy from his throne as he did countless times, lurking in and out of the night trying to survive. He did not know who he was or his people but he only knew since he moved to this part of town he had secretly crossed paths with this seemingly homeless, dirty little boy with the look of desperation in his eyes. He would be just the one he needed to learn the ends and outs of this city of Gary.

Sloth got his name because his mother said he was too lazy to come out on his own, so the doctors had to force him out and he was true to his name ever since. You would think that a man in a deadly street game in parts unknown to him would do his homework, would build up his clientele and do the necessary work of reading resumes' of the people he recruited to do his bidding. But, he did not and he didn't see why he would have to when they were weaklings like this dirty riff-raff of a little boy to do his work for him.

He brought one person with him to these unknown parts and that was his brother Goon. Goon did all the work and he had sent him out to recruit the little homeless boy to be their worker.

Sloth nudged his brother, and pointed towards the little boy who was hopping over fences, rummaging through garbage cans for food, "Go get that little Nigga!"

Goon left out of their downstairs apartment in search of him. Goon shook his head in spite of his brother. He told his brother they should get together and feel out for workers themselves, to keep their business airtight with only them two. But his brother's laziness has always been his hindrance, he had always sought out to devour the weak instead of the strong. Which is what they needed especially in these unfamiliar territories. But, he did what he was told like always and tried to catch up with the little nigga.

Ebah slowed down as he detected someone following him he ducked behind a dumpster in the alley, he held on tight to all of his senses he was fully aware of who was coming for him and why. He watched through the crack between the building and the dumpster as Goon looked both ways to see which way he went. Ebah pulled out a half-eaten burger he found in someone's garbage he unwrapped it noisily as he gave away his whereabouts. He placed the burger to his mouth as Goon came around the corner. Smack, the hamburger flew onto the pavement.

Ebah jumped up and pulled out a knife he stood in an attack stance, "Whoa, whoa little man calm down. I meant no disrespect, but I hate to see a young bull like you eating somebody else's garbage. I got someone who wants to meet you, Goon told him pulling out a wade of cash peeling him off a couple of 20's.

Ebah hesitantly put his blade away and grabbed the money from his hand and counted it, "My time is money." he said placing the forty dollars in his pocket.

Goon chuckled, "This might have been the smartest or the dumbest decision my brother has ever made." he said under his breath.

"Man, are we going to go to this meeting of the minds or are we going to shoot the shit in the alley all night? As you can see you interrupted my dinner and a growing boy like to me needs to keep up his strength. Too many vultures out here in these streets."

Goon chuckled again, "Alright, little man you got it!"

Ebah followed his lead as he led him to Sloth.

## Chapter 4

Goon lead Ebah into the downstairs apartment, as usual, Sloth was playing video games and on Facebook lying to some unsuspecting chick about his status in life. Ebah's jaw clenched as he came face to face with his devil. The instinct to pull out his gun he had in his socks depleted as he controlled his temper.

Sloth didn't even take his eyes off his phone as he put the game remote down. "What's your name, little nigga?" Sloth questioned

Ebah looked around at Goon, "I thought you said he was your brother? Why doesn't he know your name then?"

Goon chuckled again.

Goon's chuckle made him look up and put down his phone. Goon saw that the little man's demand for respect was lost to Sloth. So, he spoke up, "What is your name little man?" Goon asked as he set down next to his brother. Goon had always told Sloth that every black male didn't like to be called nigga, even if it was from another black male.

"Ebah!"

"What you do, teach this little mother fucker how to be uppity like you? He said to his brother.

Goon hunched up his shoulders.

Sloth looked at the little boy and despite his stand for respect, he still saw him as a weakling here to do what he wanted him to do. "Respect is given when it is earned," he told Ebah.

"Okay, then what's your name little nigga?"

Goon doubled over in laughter and couldn't stop himself. Sloth and Ebah stared each other down, which leads to Sloth easing the tension between them with a smirk.

Ebah let his face relax as he watched the man start back playing his game. Goon hit Sloth and pointed back to Ebah, Sloth waved his hand at him as if he was bugging him. Goon got up and motioned for Ebah to follow him to the kitchen.

Ebah shook his head this dude was too lazy to even tell him what he brought him here for, he was only here because he summoned him.

Goon pulled out three steaks, cut up some onion and bell pepper, he seasoned them and put them all in the oven to cook. Ebah ate his actions up not because he was hungry but because he never saw a man cook before. He would have to watch Goon closely to learn from him. Goon then gave him a couple of apples to satisfy his hunger until dinner was ready.

"Look, I'm not going to bullshit you, we-Naw-he told me to bring you here because he wants someone who knows the hood to move product and to bring boys your age that need to make money to him. Now, I don't condone him bringing kids your age into this game, so that is between you and him if you do it."

"He paying?"

"I'll make sure of it." Goon gave him his word

"What will he be doing?" Ebah asked

"Ump, the same thing his lazy ass is doing now?"

"What will you be doing?"

"In the trenches with you, Young Bull."

"Then let the recruiting begin," Ebah said savoring the delicious sweetness of the apples. That night as Ebah watched Goon raise his palms up to the sky and bless his food just like him. He peered over at Sloth, he devoured his food without praying over it, scoffing at his brother because he did.

Ebah found a new interest in Goon and it wasn't watching his soul leave his body.

## Chapter 5

"Are you serious? Sloth, this little boy has been risking his life and his freedom for weeks now. You are telling me that you can't remove the fucking clothes out of the third bedroom to accommodate him? Damn, to get him off of the street." Goon said heatedly in one of their many arguments about Ebah. Slowly Goon was seeing a monster grow in his brother, not that he wasn't one in the first place. However, now he had reached an all-time low. Getting this kid to recruit other homeless kids his age and younger. He became lazier and lazier by the minute. The only things he did himself was consumed food and drink, sleep, shit and wash his ass.

"Bro, I'm not moving my clothes for his dusty ass." Sloth laughed as he tried to push past his brother.

Goon stood like a statue, unmoving and placed his hand on his brother's chest. Sloth had no choice but to stop in his tracks, "I'm saying yo, Young Bull has brought you in a lot of money and we are 5 strong because of him. You have a walk-in closet now that you wouldn't even have if it wasn't for his so-called dusty ass. It would be in your best interest to protect one of your biggest assets. He's an easy target living out there. At least call Pam to hook him up with an apartment under a false name."

"Hell Naw, that bitch still trying to make me take a DNA test for her son. I don't even go to the doctor for my damn self, I sure as hell not going to confirm shit for her. Fuck that shit!" he told him moving his way around his brother plopping down on the couch to catfish some more females, he grabbed his phone.

"On the other hand, Sloth said looking up from his phone, tell that little nigga he can stay here. As long as he makes sure this shit stays clean and he's moving all of my shit out of my closet by his damn self. Then he can have the third room." Sloth returned to his phone. He had just found out a way to be even lazier. Goon left every other weekend to see his kids so Sloth didn't have a choice but to clean up and cook for himself. God forbid they ran into a problem Ebah couldn't handle himself while Goon was gone. Sloth didn't want to deal with any of that, it was beneath him, he was here just to collect money and spend it.

Goon smirked just the mention of Pam's name had that lazy ass negro in a frenzy. He got what he wanted and was satisfied that Ebah was off the street.

"When I get back, man we need to have a meeting. I'm not feeling having these little ass kids selling dope for us. That needs to change if anything we need to be mentoring them and helping them get off the street and get their asses back in school."

"You can have a meeting with your damn self. These little niggas are easy to control and plus you don't have to pay them much. Just little bit of dough will keep their asses happy. These older niggas will cause too many problems and would want more money than I'm willing to give."

Goon sucked his teeth, "You not wanting to do shit Sloth is going to be your downfall. Mark my words, Bro!" He said and walked off leaving his brother mumbling bullshit to himself.

Ebah smirked as he shut the bathroom door flushed the toilet and washed his hands. He walked out the bathroom and walked towards the door," I'm out Good, he said reaching for the doorknob.

Goon came walking down the hall, "Young Bull, he called after him.

"What's up, Good?" Ebah had started calling him Good instead of Goon because he saw that his heart was good.

"You don't need to be out in those streets. With all these killings going on, I would hate for something to happen to you out there."

"Naw, man I'm good." He told him opening the door.

"I'm not taking no for an answer. So go get your shit from wherever you stashing it at and your bedroom will be ready about time you get back."

Ebah just shook his head.

"I mean it, Young Bull, bring your ass back. Don't have me come looking for you."

Ebah sucked his teeth, "Aight man, I will be back.

True to both of their words when Ebah came back his
room was ready.

## Chapter 6

"You need anything before I leave?"

"Naw, I'm good."

"Look, Goon said coming all the way into Ebah's room and shutting the door, don't let that lazy mother fucker order you around. And between me and you, I want you to start replacing the young dudes with some older ones. They don't need to be out in these streets. They still have a chance. Find out who is going to school, who is not."

"I got you!" he said with a smile on his face. Goon was a good dude he just happened to be loyal to a messed up individual.

That night when Goon left, Ebah did everything that Sloth told him to do, even cook and brought the man his plate.

Ebah stood there watching him out of the corner of his eye. He watched him nod off. A smile crept across his face. It was time.

Splash, a bucket of ice cold water thrown on his face awakened him, "What the fuck?" Sloth barked as he felt the tightness of the ropes around his wrist and ankles. He struggled with the ropes, twisting and turning in complete darkness.

"Ebah! Ebah!" he hollered out.

A lighter flicked on reveling Ebah's sinister grin, he held the flame in front of his face to let Sloth get a glimpse of a different side of him. That side scared the shit out of Sloth.

"Untie me." Sloth demanded

"Now, why would I do that?" Ebah asked as he stood to grab his weapon of choice.

"I swear to Go-, little nigga if you don't untie me."

Ebah cracked the whip and slashed him across his feet. Instantly blood appeared, the whip had razors wedge into the leather.

"Stop being so disrespectful, Nigga! Don't swear to God. God doesn't have shit to do with a lazy ass man like you."

"Fuck You." Sloth said through his pain.

"I remember momma telling daddy, "You should never have an addiction you can't afford. He never listened." He swung the whip making it kiss its target, leaving a bloody trail on Sloth's legs.

"Urgggggggggggghhhhhhh, Mother fuck me!" Sloth hollered out.


"He never listened. She's dead because he didn't listen. And he's dead because he took his sin out on her."

"I didn't kill your Pops, Little Nigga."

" Stop interrupting my story, Little nigga. Ebah said as he walked back and forth in front of him, swinging the whip from side to side, "And I had to kill him because he tried to shut out her wisdom by killing her. You know you never once questioned me about my name. You never once wanted to know if Ebah was even my real name. You never once asked who I was or where I came from. Just too fucking lazy to even do follow up questions. Well, let me introduce myself. Seven was my birth name but EBAH is my rebirth name. And at 9 my Evil Brain killed my father because he had taken my source for my Angel Heart. My mother!"

And you mother fucker was the reason behind him killing her, of course, he shouldn't have stolen from you to feed his habit. But, you also had a choice and you chose not to go hunt down a man that despite his habit was bigger than you and probably would have given you a struggle. No, your lazy ass just like him chose to take the easy route. To feed off of a helpless God-fearing woman that was in love with a junky.

But, I listened to my mother. I developed an addiction I could afford." He told him as he swung his razor blade embedded whip across his face.

"In fact my addiction was free. It is also freeing. Blood of evil men was my addiction. I could lie and say I was killing in the name of the lord." He said swinging the whip again tearing Sloth's flesh, pieces of it hanging and falling to the floor.

"But how could I, when the Lord is peace. The Lord is love. I don't kill in the name of the Devil. Even though he would be pleased of the bloodshed but he would slit his demonic throat over the reasons behind my killings. And before you there were many and after you, there will be plenty." He cracked the whip once more wrapping it around Sloth's neck and yanking the whip so hard the chair tumbled over and Sloth's head tumbled over with it.

Ebah left the apartment leaving his father's phone right next to Sloth's body right on the video message Sloth had sent his father four years ago.

TakeOver Publishing

# Prodosia

# By

# Avorey Washington

"But if you have bitter jealousy (envy) and contention (rivalry, selfish ambition) in your hearts, do not pride yourselves on it and thus be in defiance of and false to the Truth.

This [superficial] wisdom is not such as comes down from above but is earthly, unspiritual (animal), even devilish (demoniacal).

For wherever there is jealousy (envy) and contention (rivalry and selfish ambition), there will also be confusion (unrest, disharmony, rebellion) and all sorts of evil and vile practices." James 3:14-16

## Chapter 1

Quinton Marcellus Greene stands in his full-length mirror giving himself the once over. He squints while adjusting his custom-made silk tie. He wasn't into the fancy custom clothing, but he knew this was something he would have to get used to. Fancy suits, fancy ties sent a message. A well-dressed man could walk into a room, and demand respect without even saying a word. The body language of a man in a suit could convey mystery that would make any and every one want to inquire who this person was.

Quinton or Q-as known to his friends didn't like being in the spotlight. Q was the type to move in silence and the fewer people who knew what moves he was making, the better. But given the type of work he was in, he would have to grow out his anti-social ways.

At the tender age of twenty-seven, he has accomplished more than he ever thought possible. A year ago he graduated from college with a degree in business. A month after that he landed a dream job at one of the top advertising firms in the Chicago and Northwest Indiana area. He bought a house in the suburbs and pretty much worked hard and kept a low profile.

While adjusting his cuff-links he feels a hand gently brush his shoulders. A beautiful Creole woman who is magazine cover ready stands before him with an emotionless face. Their eyes meet for a moment and he smirks while twirling his index finger around indicating he wanted to see her model for him. The woman tilts her head in a defiant way, before finally giving him the show he requested.

Just as she begins her private show, Quinton's cell phone rings. The Creole woman reaches for his phone and sees the name "E-MONEY" on the display screen.

"Your side bitch is calling", she says rolling her eyes and sucking her teeth while handing him the phone.

Quinton stops fidgeting with his cuff-link long enough to answer the call. Edward who's known as E-Money in the streets is Quinton's childhood friend. They go back like receding hairlines even to this day, despite the different paths they chose in life. While Q took the path of college absorbing education for his bright future. Edward did the only thing he knew and grew up around, he got his education in the streets.

To Quinton his friendship with Edward was everything. No matter how many people clung to Quinton through his travels in life, E-Money was the only person's intentions he never had to question. When times became rough and Q needed some extra money for his family, it was Edward who put him on in the drug game. He put him under his wing and introduced him to all the right people.

When Quinton got accepted into college with a full scholarship, E-Money threw him a going away party. He went all out for his homeboy. E-Money was happy for all of

Quinton's accomplishments school wise, except when he met Q's then at the time college girlfriend Geneviève.

Edward usually could finesse women, but not Geneviève. They despised each other from the first meeting-literally. It was close to the end of the semester during Q and Glo's junior year, and they were studying intensely. Edward had arrived on campus unannounced and had brought a harem of women to Q's dorm room. So anytime Edward called or came to visit Q on campus if Geneviève was around-Quinton was put in an awkward position, to say the least. But despite his college girlfriends warnings he still hung around Edward any chance he got. Quinton felt an undying loyalty to Edward that no one would ever understand.

In the midst of the phone conversation, Quinton never took his eyes off the woman with him. He gave his best friend a barrage of one-word answers and grunts while watching. She watched Quinton watch her, as she rolled her eyes and sighed. He continued to give hand motions for her to twirl so he could check her out.

She wore a shimmering glitter print evening dress that had an eye-catching design. A backless thin spaghetti strap V-neck dress that showed a fair amount of skin. Most dresses this woman wore would just hug her curves, this dress held them hostage.

Quinton hung up the phone, placing it in his suit jacket while focusing back on the woman. Now having his full attention again, the woman smirked as she twirled for him a second time. She makes a pose that shows off the charming side slit in the long skirt of the dress.

She notices his hungry eyes trail down her long leg and into a pair of Louboutin T Strap Pumps. He nods in approval as he finally stops fidgeting with his cuff-links. Runnings his hands along his mid-section as he turns from side to side in the mirror again, he looks to her for her sanction.

"So what do you think Glo?", Quinton asks while

posing playfully.

Only being slightly amused by his attempt at humor, she gives a minor smile and helps him with his suit jacket on. Taking a moment she walks around him, inspecting him from head to toe. She steps back, folds her arms, and excessively taps the toe her expensive heel against the hard-wood floor.

"I suppose this will have to do, there's only so much molding I can do with the materials given. I'm trying to create an Idris Elba but the final result is Lil Rel", Glo says as she winks at Quinton.

Glo is the given nick-name of Quinton's fiancée Geneviève Kalis Lonor. They both met freshmen year in college. Geneviève was fancy and a very prestigious snob, but if you got passed all that she had all the charm of a southern belle. Standing at six feet, with a good tone athletic body with a thickness in all the right places. She wasn't the normal type of girl who turned heads with her beauty, no, in fact, she broke necks.

## Chapter 2

When God, the universe, fate, or whatever laws f attraction you believe in-decides to throw a curveball, there is no curvier ball than the union of these two. Glo with her captivating beauty could, in fact, be a professional model, but only did it part-time to put herself through college. While her beau Q, who only stands five foot eight, and who is average looking at best. Far as his physical attributes, he isn't out of shape-but going to gym two times a week couldn't hurt him either.

After checking his watch, he pats himself down one last time and exits the bedroom with Glo not far behind. As they exit the front door of their home, Q takes a moment to admire the sultry walk of his fiancée. She feels his gaze and stops her strut and clears her throat.

"Mr. Greene."

"Yes, Miss Lonor."

She continues her strut in a hurried fashion to the

car, "I will not entertain any of your shenanigans on the way to this gala."

"Who me?" he says entering the car and starting it.

"Yes, you."

In a horrible southern accent he replies, "Well Miss Lonor, you need not worry about me. No, ma'am, there will be no shenanigans from the likes of me. I shall be the best gentleman ever. My name is Mr. Greene, but my balls are as blue as the ocean-as the day is long."

He tips an imaginary hat on his head, Glo rolls her eyes and checks her make up in the car visor mirror. For most of the car ride they have ridden in silence, the only sound is the random rap songs that come on the radio.

Glo occasionally steals glances at Q while he's driving. In society's eyes, someone like him should never be given the time of day by someone like her. Eyeing him up and down, she cuts her eyes for a moment and shakes her head with a smile. She thinks back to the two moments that bonded them for a lifetime as she plays with her engagement ring on her finger.

## Chapter 3

As fate would have it they saw it each other frequently during their college years. Geneviève was a hardcore socialite, her looks opened doors often for her. To most, she was an ice queen, ruthless with an alluring smile and captivating eyes. Quinton was quite the opposite, if he didn't speak you didn't know he existed. He was silent as the 'k' in knife and liked his life that way, but he still crossed paths with Geneviève.

One night Q snuck in the campus football stadium, as he always did to have a drink from a long week of studies. On this particular night, Geneviève was there as well entertaining her flavor of the week, a pretty boy with a questionable rep. Things didn't go as planned for the young man, long story short Q watched him die a slow agonizing death with a stiletto heel lunged in his throat.

Quinton found himself the only witness for a murder case turned self-defense that was mysteriously swept under the rug. Even then that still didn't stop Geneviève from keeping an eye on him. All of her low key stalking paid off when she caught Quinton in the middle of a drug deal. To sum it up, she confronted him about the dirt she had on him and now they both had dirt on each other. And that is how these two came to be, thick as thieves-and secretly joined at the hip.

## Chapter 4

Quinton is driving on I-80/94, randomly switching lanes when need be to avoid getting caught behind a Sunday driver on a Friday night.

"Quinton, you've been moving product since I've known you. Do you ever contemplate giving up that lifestyle? You know, especially since we are more than capable of living a comfortable life."

She notices his jaw clenches and his grip tightens on the steering wheel. The question lingers in the air like a bad stench. There was very little she didn't love about him, except a few things. He never disrespected her and always treated her like a lady. But despite his good treatment of her, from time to time she did love to ruffle his feathers and get a rise out of him.

She could deal with his moments of being closed off. But Geneviève despised and envied his way to blend in and not be noticed. She envied his ability to either be a fly on the wall or disappear in a blink of an eye. Both things she couldn't do because of her stand out in a crowded beauty. Plus toss in the fact of he was good at mind games, you never knew what Quinton was thinking until he let you know.

"Of course not. Are you crazy, stop living this fast money lifestyle-and live a boring mundane life?", he says with a smirk.

"Excuse me? Boring and mundane life?"

"Yes, boring.", he chuckles while switching lanes. "Give up all the excitement of the game and the excitement that it offers? And live off a bullshit pay of being in advertising. And surely you're not happy with living off an assistant farter's salary. Geneviève Lonor assistant fart-oligist, living the dream."

She playfully slaps his arm, "I hate it when you refer to my job as that. I'm an assistant anesthesiologist. And as far as that boring life with me...that's bullshit and you know it."

"Yes, it would. I wouldn't be able to have all the sex I wanted. Or even a ménage à trois."

At this moment, this was one of the things Geneviève loathed about Quinton. It was times like these she couldn't tell if he was serious or playfully teasing her. She prided herself on being able to read a man, but at times she felt illiterate with him.

"So you really want a threesome? Because I can arrange that", she asked while digging in her handbag.

"Is that so?"

"Yep, I have a friend. An old friend named Retta. Trust me, we fooled around back in college and she will blow you away."

Geneviève pulls a concealable Beretta out of her handbag, and lightly places the barrel of it in his lap. Quinton shows no fear or emotion, he continues to drive without so much as taking his eyes off the road. When she doesn't get the desired reaction, the pistol is tucked away nicely back in her handbag. The rest of the ride is in silence, both of them in their own little worlds. There are moments when she secretly steals looks at him wanting to start engaging in conversation, but she fights that urge.

## Chapter 5

They finally make it off the highway and drive through Miller, Indiana. Quinton ventures down Lake Street so he can take in the festive art vibe proudly displayed. From there he speeds down a few side streets until he winds up on Montgomery St. After that he slowly rolls down Oak Avenue to admire the beach. He loved how at night Miller Beach looked like the perfect scene from a horror movie, even down to the one light that flickered repeatedly in the dead of night.

Geneviève smiles and caresses Quinton's hand as he drives by the Aquatorium. This place holds different meanings for the both of them. For Quinton a rush of memories that include childhood and his best friend E-Money. For Geneviève, it's the place where Quinton proposed to her. He had gone out of his way to have the upper level of the Aquatorium decked out with lights and floral arrangements. Everything from a personal chef, that cooked her favorite meal-down to the music the rented disc jockey played.

Quinton pulls up in front of the Marquette Pavilion where he is greeted by a valet. Uneasy, he looks around at a few others arriving at this gala. After receiving the valet ticket, he tucks it away in his suit jacket. Geneviève walks around the car and pauses, she takes the time to look him over once more brushing away any lent she may have missed at the house.

They view the people around them for a moment. Glo and Q whisper jokes among themselves and admire the attires of those entering the gala ahead of them.

"Well, well, well don't you two look prom night fly. Y'all brought out the good Sunday clothes I see", says a husky male voice.

Turning around they are greeted by Quinton's best friend Edward as he stands there with a rather uncouth woman. The best friends greet each other in their own way, with a handshake they've been doing since grade school. Geneviève manages a fake but pleasant smile for the woman accompanying E-Money.

"Geneviève, a pleasure as always", Edward says mockingly as he sucks his teeth.

"You look handsome tonight Edward. Casket sharp in fact," she replies.

Geneviève almost vomits at the thought of saying anything positive to E-Money. She always felt uncomfortable the way he eyed her, like a wolf salivating over raw meat. In her view, vibes of resentment for her and the things Q had accomplished, oozed through his pores. At times she even thought if it was possible he would rape her or worse at the first chance an opportunity presented itself. Over time she always let Quinton know it was something about him she never trusted.

"I look casket sharp huh?" he says while smiling slyly.

"Yes, you do. In fact, it's a shame that you're not in one now and that this isn't your funeral we're attending." Geneviève retorts with a deadpan expression on her face.

E-Money smirks and nods his head slightly at Geneviève's statement. Quinton eyes the building tension and steps in to ease it. He lets E-Money know he will catch up with him inside a bit. Having been outwitted by Geneviève he eyes her up and down one last time before strolling off with his date.

Once they are out of earshot Geneviève turns to Quinton.

"Ugh, every time he's around-he makes my skin crawl. And every time he speaks my name it upsets my soul. I told you I don't trust him, Quinton. He's a snake and he's jealous of you. Don't be blinded by your loyalty."

Quinton rubs his chin, "Are you done? Do you need more time to finish this tantrum out here, or are we good?"

When Geneviève is ready she clears her throat, giving the signal that she's ready to finally go inside.

## Chapter 6

Geneviève inhales deeply and smiles as they walk into the pavilion. She stands there for a moment, her arm locked with Quinton's taking in the ambiance. For a moment she scans the room, watches guests venture into the lounge area downstairs to enjoy finger foods and drinks. The upper gallery is adorned with spectacular white, black, grey and indigo accents. Violet up lighting splashed all along the walls, giving a radiant tone.

As the music from the live band playing rushes at them, they slowly walk further in with fake social smiles ready to be flashed at a moment's notice. They give the occasional head nod and wave as a greeting to associates. Glo was at home in these sorts of social environments, as Q reviled them with a lukewarm passion. He never was jealous of the way she could socially work a room, he let her shine and use one of her best strengths.

They seat themselves at an empty table that's not too far off in the back but was still accessible to the dance floor.

The indigo up lights set the atmosphere for the party, they watched guests dance to their heart content. Both of them taking notice of the well put together table arrangement. Geneviève spends twenty minutes alone talking Quinton's ear off about the diamond studded flower vases and the silk black table clothes. He took the time to make a mental note that she may want something similar at their future wedding.

This elegant gala is filled with a who's who of Illinois and Indiana, with even a few big shots from various parts of Michigan. Anyone you can think of that's on the books officially and unofficially. From mayors, alderman's, school city council members and legal and illegal businessmen. High ranking members of various divisions of law enforcement, college chancellors, and a few highly favored street pharmacist.

"You know what I like about events like this", Glo says while sipping from her wine glass.

"If you say one more damn word about these fucking table-cloths", Q says while eating.

The meal of the evening consists of gourmet roasted chicken on top of rice with a side of asparagus. He looks over at his fiancée as she stares at him coldly. If looks could kill Quinton would be dead for the next two lifetimes. Laughter escapes him as he shakes his head.

"No, I don't know what you like about parties like this Glo. I really don't see the big deal, it's just a social circus. A bunch of overpaid and possibly dirty city officials, mixed with law enforcement that could be dirty as well. Lots of businessmen who put on a good front and bring their wives- while their mistresses are somewhere hidden in the crowd. And the icing on the cake is the fact their favorite drug dealers are all here within arm's reach, in case someone wants to have some nose candy or whatever their pleasure. So enlighten me about the fun, besides the added pleasure of laughing at some of their choice of suits."

"Actually that is the fun part", Glo says while finishing off the last of her wine.

"What? The fact that their all dressed up?"

"Absolutely. With them all dressed up, you can't tell

the difference between the politicians and the drug dealers. The fun is in guessing who is who."

Glo snobbishly toasts her empty wine glass with a smile, as Q chuckles to himself at her brand of humor. The evening continues on in a splendid fashion, as they drink and laugh. A waiter brings another bottle of wine to the table, just as a gentleman approaches the couple.

The gentleman stands with one hand on his mid-section as he bends over, and whispers a message to the both of them. They both graciously smile at the gentleman as he takes his leave. After finishing her current glass of wine, they make their exit out one of the doors leading to the patio. As they exit through the doors, an uncomfortable feeling overcomes Glo. She glances over her shoulder to see E-Money staring at the both of them with a spiteful expression.

## Chapter 7

The cool night winds playfully run along the shoulders of Glo, causing her to shiver a bit. Quinton puts his suit jacket around her as they venture further out onto the patio. A seductive woman smiles and lightly waves for the two to come in her direction. The unknown woman graciously asks them to have a seat at the awaiting table.

A few moments pass and a waiter brings a bottle of champagne and three glasses. As the waiter leaves they hear the sound of a slow deliberate clap coming in their direction from behind. Glo and Q turn around to see a tall, well-tailored dark skin man. The mystery man stands there with a childlike grin on his face, as he is surrounded by three bodyguards. Soon as they stand up, the source of the clapping courteously asks them to sit by nodding his head.

"Well, well Quinton or shall I call you Q-as all the boys do", his deep baritone voice says.

Quinton stands up and shakes the hand of one of the most cryptic men he will ever come to meet or know in his life. The mystery man removes his hat and reaches out to kiss the hand of Glo.

"Quinton is fine or whatever you prefer Mr. McCall", Q says sitting back down.

Troy Mathius McCall.

Standing face to face with him, and seeing his gracious alluring smile, you would think Billy Dee Williams had a darker twin brother. He was a smooth talker from the old school. Even his enemies would say he was one of the fairest and honest men you'll ever meet in the drug game.

He was one of the humblest high profile criminals that stayed low key and businessmen in the Chicago and Northwest Indiana area. No one has any real info or history on the man, they just know he exists. When he wants to be found, he is found, and when he wants to disappear he does that. For all his legal business ventures he is known as more than fair with a business partner. Most people feel as if they have had dinner with President Obama if Mr. McCall wanted to do business with you.

But that was the legal business venture version of

Troy McCall or T-Mac as many of his men called him behind his back. The underworld version of him is another world of pain and misery. Many have suffered when they have had the unfortunate pleasure of being the target of his wrath. Only a few have lived and been able to spread the word of what he's capable of, especially if he has to get his own hands dirty.

Mr. McCall sits, crosses his legs as he pulls out a Cuban cigar out his suit jacket. One of his bodyguards lights it, as Glo removes a small envelope from her handbag and slides it across the table. As Troy inspects the envelope, Q tries not to let his curiosity show that he is semi bothered by the action that just happened. For a moment he sees a cold stare on his fiancée' face, she stares at him as if they are strangers.

Once Mr. McCall has finished with the envelope, he passes it off to his bodyguard and nods him away. He smiles and stares at both Quinton and Geneviève as he puffs his cigar.

"I'll cut to the chase. Quinton, you've worked for me

since you were in high school. You and Edward, good workers. You both have different work ethics. I respect a man with a good work ethic."

"Thank you sir", Quinton says as he rubs his chin. He shifts in his chair a bit, still uneasy about the exchange between Glo and Troy.

"Son relax, you're sitting there like a long tail cat in a room full of rocking chairs." Mr. McCall opens the bottle of champagne and pours some for all three of them. "Long story short son I want to expand your reach within my organization. This is what I wanted to talk to you about tonight."

"Expand?"

"That's right. You know how to maneuver in a room of sharks and businessmen. Be it legal or illegal. You don't sweat under pressure, you don't let money persuade you- and most of all you're loyal. I need those kinds of qualities in my close inner circle."

Q nods as he rubs his chin, "Just how much of an expansion are we talking?"

"Trust me, son, it will be well worth it. A lot of traveling from time to time", Troy says while pouring more champagne in his glass.

"With all due respect sir, I'm very gracious for the offer. But if a lot of travel is involved that may interfere with my day job."

Mr. McCall smirks at Quinton while sipping champagne. Moments later he motions for Q to look through the nearest pavilion window. Quinton plays along and follows Troy's lead. Looking through the window he sees his boss sitting at a table with the mayor and a few questionable figures laughing and drinking.

"Thank you for the offer Mr. McCall-I'll think it over and reach out to you", Quinton says as he stands up.

Troy shockingly looks over at Geneviève with disbelief written on his face, as he shakes Quinton's hand. A guard comes over and whispers into his boss's ear, and takes leave just as fast as he arrives. Q buttons his suit jacket and begins in the direction of the door leading back inside, when he notices Geneviève is still sitting at the table.

"Give us a moment Mr. Greene if you will. I've received some urgent news of the medical kind-and I'm aware that your fiancée is in the medical field." Mr. McCall eyes Geneviève for a moment, before turning his attention back to Q. "I would like to bounce something...", Mr. McCall stops mid-sentence when he notices that Quinton is no longer there. Geneviève turns around to see Quinton gone, and turns back to Mr. McCall attempting to mask her anger at his sudden disappearance.

"He certainly does know how to make an exit, doesn't he", Troy says while sipping champagne as Glo smiles awkwardly.

## Chapter 8

Quinton was uneasy about how comfortable Geneviève was with Mr. McCall-but kept his cool about it. They had met a few times over the last two years, but nothing major. In his eyes, they never got to the point of where Mr. McCall would want to ask her for personal advice, especially for being so well connected. For him it didn't fit right at all, there was an angle he was missing.

Glo was only an assistant anesthesiologist, not to say she wasn't qualified to answer anything medical, but why ask her when he knew for a fact there were more qualified people in the pavilion to ask. People who were far, far above Glo's pay grade, and had their own practices, that he knew Mr. McCall golfed with.

The full moon shone down brightly onto the beach, illuminating the water making it look like a sea of never-ending darkness. Q stood on the top level of the Aquatorium admiring the view. He stood there thinking about Mr. McCall's offer, the pros, and cons of it. He also still was thinking of the angle he was missing with Glo and Mr. McCall. He was almost at a formal conclusion when the sound of a camera phone snapping a picture broke his concentration.

"I swear nigga I'm going to find me a painter to paint this shit", says a voice filled with laughter from behind him.

Quinton shakes his head as he turns around to see E-Money with a bottle of liquor.

"What's wrong the open bar wasn't good enough for you E?"

"Shit you know me Q, sometimes I like to bring my own shit. You dig? Even when the main party is going on, there's always a moment to start another party."

Unlike Q, E-Money was loud and flashy- he wanted everyone to know who he was and what he was about. He was a local businessman, who owned his car detailing shop as well as a few other businesses. If you didn't respect him as a man, then he was the type to make sure you feared him like a bitch.

"What's good with you E-Mo.?"

Edward hands Quinton a bottle of Cîroc.

"My nigga I'm good, a party is going on, good food and drink. Bitches dancing everywhere. Life is chill. I should be asking you what's good, you the one over here all alone looking into the darkness and shit like some sad depressing ass painting."

Quinton takes a hard drink from the bottle and lets the bottle bounce on his thigh for a moment.

"Q, man I never got why you were always so hung up on this place. Like I get it's all romantic and shit, I remember fucking a chick over there in the corner on a blanket."

Quinton drinks from the bottle again and replies, "It's the architecture man. The set-up, at the right time you can see the sunset, and it looks like the sun is melting into the water. You know this used to be a bathing house right..... "

E-Money takes the bottle back from Quinton.

"Yeah yeah, I know back in 1922 this fucking placed opened. And the damn Pavilion was finished two years later. Yeah fool, I know all about this. Shit thank you Mr. History of Marquette Park. Knowing your book smart ass you can probably tell me the first nigga to fuck on the beach.

They look at each other and bust out laughing.

"Fuck you E", Quinton says wiping tears out his eyes.

"Back in the summer of '22, a young Jethro Jenkins came down here with Lakeisha Mae and they fucked on the beach. This has been your moment in Marquette Park history", E-Money says in a white announcer voice.

A moment of nostalgia sneaks up on the both of them as they laugh. They talk about the beach, and the first time they met here in elementary school. They discuss the different paths they took in life, which led them to the here and now.

"Jesus E-Mo, you got like six kids now?"

"Six and one on the way", Edward takes a long swig from the bottle. "I mean we all can't be like you and go to college and find an uppity black snowflake and settle down."

"So that's like four baby mommas now?"

"Yea. And we ain't out here to discuss my dick

slinging skills. Why you out here Mr. History of Marquette?"

They chuckle at the joke for a moment. E-Mo pulls out a black and mild and offers, Q declines and leans against the stone balcony.

"So apparently Mr. McCall wants to expand my reach in the enterprise."

Quinton can sense the change in Edward's body language and vibe but says nothing as he takes another drink from the bottle.

"Oh, that's what he on. Last time you and I were shooting the shit, you were talking about getting out the game. You still think that?", E-Money asks while blowing smoke.

"Is that the question of the night? You are like the second person to ask me that."

"I'm just saying Q, I saw you and your snow bunny out there with him. Looking like a scene in Godfather or the fucking Soprano's and shit."

"She isn't a snow bunny. I told you about that E, she's creole. And I don't know where I stand at the moment.

Some days I want out, other days I get high off the rush."

"Whatever, she light enough to possibly pass for white bruh-that's all I'm saying. And you better keep an eye on her like I been told you. I peeped game, she was out there a while talking to T-Mac. She was still there before I left to come to find you."

"The fuck? How much did you see? You stalking mofo's now?"

They both laugh as Q hands the bottle back to Edward. Silence joins them and makes this situation awkward. Although they stand at arm's length physically, mentally there are as close as the sun to the earth.

"So what he offer you Q?"

"No idea, I left before he could go into detail."

"You know I been grinding for him since high school. And up until about two years ago, he just not started letting me get a little shine."

Quinton leans up against the concrete pillar with his back to Edward.

"What do you mean, let you shine Ed? You own a

strip club out here in Miller, and you have your car shop. Far as I know you been the man."

"Well, I'm glad to know that you feel that way, my nigga."

"Always.

"Which is what's gonna make this even harder to do."

## Chapter 9

Quinton turns around to see Edward with a Glock pointed at him. E-Money takes a long drag on the cigar and tosses it.

"Listen Q, I wish I could tell you this is just business my nigga. But then I'd be lying to you, and I don't want your last thoughts of me being a liar."

"Of course I get it. Betray me like Judas did Jesus. Kill me like Cain did Abel. Do me like Bishop did Raheem in "Juice". Naw wouldn't want to add liar to that resume", Quinton says sarcastically.

"I respect that. A smart ass to the bitter end huh?"

"At this point, I just want to know why E."

Edward gets nervous for a moment and runs his hand across his neck, never once taking the gun off Quinton.

"Truth of the matter is, you got in the game to deep and too good. You out here making me look bad, and I'm the nigga who put you on. Nigga you owe me your life. Motherfuckers should be singing my praises not yours."

Quinton smirks as he leans against the concrete pillar, his hands still in visible sight.

"Wait a minute", Quinton scratches his temple for a moment. "So because I took what you taught me, and made it better. You mad now? Because you feel you should be where I am. Is that it? Bruh, I said I was considering leaving the game anyway. I got one foot in and one foot out."

"See Q that's the thing. That one foot out one foot in is what gets niggas killed. And trust me, you stuck in this shit until you die. Ain't no getting out for you, now you in this shit for life-especially if T-Mac is pulling strings for you-and having secret meetings with you."

A confused look overcomes Quinton. E-Money starts laughing uncontrollably.

"Finally for the first time, I'm finally smarter than the so-called smartest nigga in the room. Let me lay it all out for you Q. See niggas talk, you came in-made an impression. You a fair dude-all these niggas start respecting you-and shitting on me. You out here treating these little corner niggas like they matter. I got niggas on my own team, trying to see if they can get under your umbrella. You got niggas under me, trying to jump ship to your team. Which means my workers don't respect me. And if they don't respect me, then they play with my money. Shit for all I know the territory he giving you could be one of my blocks. I can't have that."

E-Money stares at Quinton hard, and like most people can't put a finger on just how he will react. Here he was gun pointed at him, and this man was cooler than a polar bear's balls in the North Pole. No begging for his life, all he got from Quinton was a vibe of utter arrogance.

Quinton takes another sip from the bottle, then says, "So because you were sloppy out in these streets, it's my fault. It's on me that I know in order to get respect you have to give it."

Edward inhales deeply, his hand in a constant state of gripping and releasing the gun.

"Don't none of that matter now. See all T-Mac sees in you is potential to be at the big table. Niggas like me get a few scraps. I work hard out here, and best I can get is he runs shit through both my businesses. That's all I am to him a duffle bag boy. Meanwhile, he's setting you up nice, pulling strings for your ass and getting you set for life. My time is now, and when I'm done with you. It'll be a matter of time for I catch T-Mac slipping and he'll get his. I'mma take over his whole empire."

"Wait! What? Setting me up how?"

Edward shakes his head at Quinton, "Nigga you think I ain't know about that situation down at school? Yeah, snowflake went straight 'single white female' on dude, killed him with her shoe and shit. T-Mac made that all go away, he pulled strings. Plus how you think you got that sweet ass job and still can move the weight you move, huh? All that is McCall-you into too deep with him, you ain't never getting out."

Quinton let everything that Edward said sink in for a moment, and just as fast as it settled new thoughts came and knocked it all away. He thought about the many times he had been to this place. The memories on the beach, the memories of the both of them playing together. Then he thought of the memories he shared at this place as a man. The moment he proposed to Geneviève and thought he would have the chance to spend the rest of his life with her.

He looks at Edward as he still points the gun at him. He sees the nervous look in his eye, his hand is shaking. He smiles slowly at his friend.

"I have to give it to you Q, you taking this all like a champ. Most niggas would have pissed their pants by now and been begging like a bitch."

Quinton bounces the bottle against his thigh again, laughing to himself, then says. "This is actually all quite poetic in a sick Shakespeare type of way if you look at it E-Mo."

"Ugh, nigga here you go, even before you die you have to sound all deep and shit. What's all poetic about you dying here? Because this is where we hung out as kids, or cause this is where you proposed to snowflake"

Quinton finishes off the last of the liquor and tosses the bottle over the balcony.

"You right, minus the part about me dying E."

"Well Q thinks of it like this, you were gonna eventually get got by someone. So it might as well be me, you not built for this street game. And if you worried about Glo, being all depressed and broken up-don't worry I'll be there to comfort her. And when I'm done having my fun with her, and breaking her- I'll put that uppity bitch in a shallow grave somewhere. It's the least I can do seeing as we boys and all. I'll make sure you have a nice funeral."

"Yeah, a nice funeral-I was just thinking the same about you. Open casket or closed? What's your choice?"

Edward's quick temper gets the best of him, gun aimed at his friend's chest he walks toward him slowly. Quinton stands there arrogantly smiling, but Edward then notices that Quinton is looking in his direction but not directly at him. His eyes seem as if they are focused on something behind him.

Just as he turns around, Quinton ducks and five shots ring out. Three of the bullets finding a home in E-Money, causing him to go over the balcony.

Quinton stands up balancing himself against the

concrete pillar, as he stares at Geneviève. She stands there with a gun at her side, with a smug look on her face.

"The hell, playing it kind of close weren't you Glo.", he says resting comfortably on the concrete balcony railing.

"I was trying to make sure I recorded all that, just in case he was going to reveal some plan or something. Plus you try walking fast and sneaking around in stilettos."

"Glo you could have taken them off."

She scoffs at his comment, "And risk getting my feet dirty. I just got a Pedi-boy bye. Now stop playing so we can go down there and find his body. I know that fall didn't kill him."

Before Quinton can give a reply everything slows down. He feels a forearm around his neck, pulling him over the balcony as another gunshot goes off. He doesn't see where it hits Glo, he just sees her go down as he falls into the darkness below.

## Chapter 10

Geneviève was right about the fall not being enough
to kill anyone. But it was enough to subdue and injure a
person. Outside the three gunshots, Edward had suffered a
broken leg. The first time he went over, he was fortunate
enough to grab the ledge, so he never hit the ground. It was
only now falling with Quinton he felt the full brunt of the
drop. On the other hand, due to his landing Quinton only
suffered what seemed to be a dislocated shoulder and a
possible concussion from hitting his head.

E-Money tried by any means to get away further into
the darkness. After two failed attempts of trying to hobble
away on one leg, he crawled along the concrete walkway
leaving a trail of blood behind. He finally stops crawling at
the oval rest area with concrete benches, near a lamp post
with a shorting light. Moments later a semi disoriented
Quinton falls to his knees beside him. No words are spoken,
just bitter looks of resentment and the sounds of both men
in pain and breathing heavy. The lamp post light flickers in

and out, making an annoying buzzing sound.

Q wipes the blood out his eyes from the head wound he has, as he hears someone approaching. The steady sound of heels clicking, send a shock through his soul. But the sound of the conversation he had with Edward, dulls that shock. The light from the lamp goes out, but when the light returns, he sees Geneviève standing over him, next to her is Mr. McCall and five bodyguards.

"Well this is a most unfortunate scene of events on a night that was meant for celebration", Mr. McCall says as he squats down between both men. The recording finally stops as Mr. McCall smiles at Edward.

"So Edward, or E-Money, you may be right. I may get mine, one day. But I know this young man you won't be around to see it. See there's nothing wrong with being hungry and ambitious, I like that. But see with little niggas like you, see you get beside yourself. See the same thing happen to your old man James, and that's how he got laid out-just like you are now. Like father like son....."

Quinton and Edward look at each other for a

moment.

"You killed his father? Quinton asks grimacing in pain.

Mr. McCall grins at the both of them.

"You know I really dig this whole best friend thing. James and I had the same thing going until he tried to double cross me-the same way Edward tried to do you. Yes, I had to lay his father out like Old Yeller. And I was hoping that Edward would learn a lesson, but apparently, the apple doesn't fall too far from the tree. But here's to hoping that when I get a hold of one old E-Money's kids, they'll be better than dad and their granddaddy was."

E-Money tries to lunge at Mr. McCall but he's too weak, at best his arm flails at him. Out of spite, Geneviève takes that opportunity to drive her heel into one of his bullet wounds.

"Well, I guess there's only one question left. Do you want an open or closed casket, Edward?"

Mr. McCall laughs at his own joke and looks between both of the men. Neither finds humor in his statement. In his last act of defiance, Edward spits blood, nailing Mr. McCall in the face. Geneviève pulls the trigger, delivering a bullet to E-Moneys head. A rage flies through Quinton who jumps up, drawing a gun from his suit jacket, only to be met by the barrel of Geneviève gun.

Quinton's pistol is aimed at Glo's shoulder. He doesn't have a direct kill shot like she does due to him still being disoriented, and blood partially blurring his vision. Geneviève aggressively drives the barrel of the gun into Quinton's forehead, while pleading with her eyes not to make her kill him. Mr. McCall cleans himself off with a handkerchief while waiting to see what will transpire between the two.

"Well, I think this is my cue to take my leave. Lover's quarrels were never much my thing. Hopefully, you and my niece can work this little situation out. And hopefully, you will still consider my offer to you Mr. Greene. Good night."

Mr. McCall walks off with three of the five bodyguards, the remaining two stay with Geneviève and Quinton. Adrenaline coursing through his veins, rage and

E-Money's words ringing in his head. Dried and fresh blood cover part of Quinton's face, and with the effect of the flickering light it gives the appearance of a demon and frightens Glo.

"You're.....his......his.... niece?!?!", a low chilling growl erupts from Q through clenched jaws.

"I'm sure you have questions, Quinton."

"YOU'RE HIS FUCKING NIECE", Q yells while his hand holding the gun shakes. His breathing becomes labored. "BITCH YOU BEEN FUCKING PLAYING ME THE WHOLE FUCKING TIME."

His emotions unchained, Quinton points his gun at her forehead and the bodyguards draw their pistols. She motions to him, and he notices the red dots on his chest. He turns to the guards before turning his attention back to Glo.

"Well, I guess we all die tonight huh? At least we casket ready," he says then swallows hard as the gun is still aimed at Glo's head.

## Chapter 11

Geneviève had never seen this side of Quinton before, she didn't know it even existed. His facial features appear devil possessed, his eyes were cold and dark.

"Q, we don't have to. We can all walk away from this tonight."

"Are you fucking serious Geneviève? If that's even your real name?

"As I said, I know you have questions, which I will answer. But I'm not putting this gun down", she says while grinding the barrel into his forehead. "At first this was all an assignment for me. My father and my Uncle Troy built an empire. Neither of them had any sons, all girls. And despite how far we have come with respect and equality for women in the real world, imagine how much tougher it is in the crime world. None of my cousins were serious about keeping the bloodline and family business going, so I wanted to prove I could. My uncle saw potential in you, figured you could be a good boss one day with the right guidance. He wanted me to keep an eye on, report to him."

Quinton lowers his gun and backs away from Glo. He lets everything she said settle in his head, as he paces back and forth. Geneviève keeps her gun trained on him, as do the bodyguards-as they listen to him mumble to himself.

"So you were his little- trained puppet sent to keep an on me", Quinton laughs as he sits on the ground next to E-Money's lifeless body. He taps him as if he will respond. "Hey E, get up man you're gonna wanna hear this shit."

Quinton struggles but finally manages to set E-Money's corpse up, leaning it against the bench they're in front of. Glo continues her story as Quinton digs around in E-Money's suit jacket until he produces a black and mild and lighter.

"Listen Q, long story short. In the beginning, no I didn't like you. You were just an assignment to prove I had what it took to be a boss in my family's eyes. But you grew me over time, and I fell for your ass. Realistically I had to be honest about my dad and uncle upholding their word about me being in charge. So for me, it was a win-win, even if I did get looked over and you became boss-I'd technically still be on the throne because we would have been married. You would have me, to help you, hold you down all that good shit. So it was a win for both of us either way it went."

Quinton coughs and exhales cigar smoke, "So I was a meal ticket. That explains a lot."

"What does that explain exactly?"

"Explains why a lot of shit went down the way it did. But more so explains why you got comfortable. I didn't want to say anything but you've picked up some weight. That's what usually happens when women find a sucker.", he says with a lighthearted laugh.

Geneviève fires two rounds off into E-Money's corpse, it shakes and slumps over to the side. Quinton looks at her crying face, it looks contorted from the flickering of the light.

"I'm sorry I just wanted to remind you that I do have a gun in my hand. And I've only picked up weight because I'm pregnant. So if I were you, I would choose your next words carefully Q."

Quinton takes a long hit off the black, and then exhales, "How many months."

"Two months."

"And when were you going to tell me."

"Later tonight. When we got home",

"Two fucking months, and......", Q begins to raise his voice.

Glo points the gun back at him. He shakes his head and takes another hit of the black.

"Listen, Quinton, you're a smart man. Do the math, do the math in which we both live happily ever after together married with a kid. Because I love you, and I mean I really love you. Not the friendly love, puppy love where bitches bust windows out. No, I mean that 'if you ever cheat on me I'll have to put you where no one can smell you' love. I would really hate to have to put one in you right now, and then explain to our child why they don't have a father around. And secondly, I'm not about that single mother life bullshit."

He laughs and throws his head back until he chokes.

"Oh my God is everyone hearing this", he turns to both the bodyguards. "Come on fellas, you know you want to laugh. You can't tell me this isn't some shit out of a damn Greek tragedy or something. Fucking Shakespeare is probably turning over in his grave laughing."

One of the bodyguards lets out a chuckle, and the other shakes his head.

"Hey E-money", Quinton shoves the corpse, "you hear this shit?" Quinton's howling laughter soon dies down. A few tears creep out in between his now barely audio chuckles. Looking over at his dead best friend. It all sinks in, and Quinton finally breaks. All the pain, mental, physical and emotional-it finally breaks him and hits him hard.

"Hey money, your grannie always said the drug game would always get us killed. Seems like your death was fast and smooth my man."

He grunts loudly in pain, struggling to stand up. Not wanting to take any chances Geneviève steps back and aims the pistol. Their eyes meet for a second, as Quinton relights his black and mild. He then turns back to the corpse of his friend.

"Meanwhile Edward looks like my death is going to be a looooong and hard one-which might involve a kid or two."

"Maybe three", Geneviève says slightly smiling while stilling pointing the gun.

Quinton exhales, and kicks Edward's corpse, "Save me a seat at the bar, and a bottle of Cîroc kid. And I'll see you in about fifty or sixty years."

Q begins walking back along the cement walkway, following the blood trail Edward left behind. Stopping for a moment, he looks over his shoulder-sees Geneviève and the bodyguards still standing where he left them.

"So is anyone going to take the possibly, new maybe someday soon to be boss to the hospital or I am going to be joining my best friend at the bar earlier than anticipated."

One bodyguard walks up and helps Quinton to a parked limo in front of the Aquatorium, and helps him inside. Moments later Geneviève climbs into the limo, they both stare at each other for what seems like an eternity.

Quinton notices she's bleeding from her shoulder and nods.

"Look at that you got shot in the shoulder, and I may have a dislocated shoulder."

Geneviève smirks, "Quite the pair, are we not?"

Quinton exhales loudly with laughter and says, "A Got damned Greek tragedy."

Author Ms. Pantha Jones's titles
Join Our VIP Mailing List to receive free books,
Merchandise,
Download her books before the rest of the world, Contests!
Just simply email her and put Join VIP Mailing list in the
subject. Mwah, who loves you baby?
ms.panthajoneslrb@gmail.com